MONA

And Other Twisted Stories

MONA

AND OTHER TWISTED STORIES

BY

COLIN HESTON

Australian Edition

HARROW AND HESTON
Publishers

Australia, New York & Philadelphia

Australian Edition

ISBN: 978-0-911577-47-1

Library of Congress Control Number: 2019955871

Cover design by Graeme Newman, based on a painting by Rosemary McKenry

Table of Contents

1. MONA

An unwelcome visit to the Museum of Old and New Art

Charon delivers
A bridge of thighs,
Of virgin souls,
Unknowable,
Where to look?
Black stone rises
Darkness beckons
Souls lost, staggering
Now a blinding iridescence
Dazzled by green,
Stabbed by an abyss from
Above and below.
Leap!
Turn and take the curve!
Which way is up?
Falling down
Charon take us back!

Look there! To left!
A man sits
Naked to the waist
Hands on knees
Marbled skin
Lifeless.
Round the corner
A quick peep,
Odour of hot breath
There they are!
Humans at last.
Alas, they are only
Bones in love.

The sound of
Four letter words
Beckons.
Is there no exit here?
Sheets of water,
Splash their universal message,
Heaven sent,
Droplets speak
The four letter words
Watered down.

2. The Tommie Felon Show

Reality TV at its finest

In Safar, 1442 A.H. a ground-breaking late night talk show was aired on Ozone TV, the new network experts predict will overtake the slowly dying cable and satellite networks of the world. The new technology is far superior to satellite because it can bounce signals back to earth by navigating them via the ozone layer around the earth so that they can be retrieved from any place in real time -- rather like the old short wave radio that found its way around the earth by hitching a ride on earth's clouds (real clouds, that is). Even more important, the Ozone layer is there to stay, not like satellites that eventually fall to earth and these days can be shot down at any time. Our TV/Internet combination offers customers a simple, basic service, with just the one channel, the Felony Channel, the most popular channel in all TV ever, and the fastest Internet service. The Internet service comes free with a subscription to the Felony Channel. This makes it far cheaper than any of the competition. It also makes the channel accessible and affordable to the poorest customers anywhere around the world.

By far the most popular show is the Tommie Felon show that premiered in Safar, 1442 A.H. (I repeat myself, a habit of all TV personalities whether in front or behind the scenes). The first episode turned out to be so popular, its viewing surpassed many of the top You Tube videos. When one considers that the Tommie Felon show runs for approximately 20 minutes, including commercials, it makes You Tube, and other competitors look pretty limited. The naysayers had warned us that our viewers would not have the attention span to stay with a twenty-minute show. How wrong they were!

We are currently in negotiations with UAE TV to release the franchise to them with the hope that they will begin broadcasting the show sometime in the fall of 1448 A.H. As part of our promotional literature for distributing the franchise of the show, we have prepared this brief account of the first record-breaking show and a little background on its basic premise. The season premiere was such an important event that we reproduce here a small piece of the transcript, slightly revised and edited.

The set for this show is modelled on the prison cells of the notorious Kilmainham Gaol in Dublin, Ireland, a classic 19th century multi-level prison, each level lined with bars of cells and railings, iron steps running up and down in the centre of the prison, and catwalks connecting each side, seemingly suspended in space. The show opens with the camera panning first with a wide angle to take in the expanse of the prison, then takes us on a quick tour of the cells while the credits appear, finally entering the cell where the moderator sits dressed in a stylized prison guard uniform, her figure accentuated just a little too much, although these days it's difficult to reach any higher level of excess. Let us just say that her appearance is one of voluptuousness, admittedly an ugly word, if it is a word, but seems to us to be quite appropriate. No doubt the producers and directors of the show spent a lot of time coming up with the costume, especially the bright green of the uniform contrasting with the dull surroundings of the prison cells, the black bars, grey blankets, and bed of galvanized iron anchored to the floor. Of course, this set is not in Ireland but constructed in the Felony Channel studio in space leased from the new Freedom Tower in New York City, on the hundredth floor.

The moderator sits at a small round table with polished chrome legs and glass top. The chairs are of black finely wrought iron, nicely crafted curves, no cushions, rather like high-class outdoor furniture. There are strict rules of conduct for the interviews. (Of course, the rules are made to be broken). There must be no touching; in fact, the guests and moderator must maintain a distance from each other of at least one foot. The guest, if a felon and currently serving time, must be shackled at all times to his or her chair and is transported from whatever prison in a high-security van, clear windows all around, a little bit like a squat version of the old Pope-mobile.

Before we proceed with the edited transcript of the first show, a word about our famous moderator is necessary in order to dispel any misunderstandings or misconceptions about what the show's basic premise is all about. We wanted a moderator who could connect easily with all classes of people (we do not use "class" in the Marxist sense but in the scientific sense), who could convey with ease an air of deep understanding of her guests and of the topics discussed. Naturally, the title of the show conveys to the audience that this is a show about criminals, what they do to their victims, and what is and should be done to them once they are caught. As even the least informed members of our audience know, Tommie Felon has been convicted on several occasions (one of them a cause célèbre when found naked except for a G-string in the President's office —we do not need to say which president—of course, this was not a crime at the time) and another was falsifying the forms required to qualify for health insurance so as to get maximum coverage to pay for a novel kind of sex change operation. Tommie received two years in prison for that felony, sentence suspended, and there have been a string of events in which she allegedly violated her probation by supposedly soliciting sex from various politicians who sent her revealing photographs of themselves, mistakenly thinking she was a prostitute. We assure you that we conducted an extensive background check (in fact we had the FBI do it for us under contract) and can say that Tommie has never prostituted herself. We admit that there must be one qualification to this postulation, which will become clear when we describe the structure of the show and its now well-known daily schedule.

The Tommie Felon show is aired Monday through Saturday at 8.00 pm. E.S.T. On Mondays, Wednesdays, and Fridays. Tommie is dressed out as herself, a voluptuous female, as we described above. On Tuesdays, Thursdays, and Saturdays, Tommie is dressed as himself, a straight, slim, mildly muscled-up male, his correction officer's jacket short sleeved to show off his upper arms, and his correction officer's pants, a slim modern cut of shorts, styled after those worn by Australian Rules Footballers, showing his lower thighs, shapely knees, and curvaceous calves. In sum, Tommie Felon is a transgendered individual whom (both he and she) we are totally convinced is able to connect with the amazingly diverse range of people who make up our audiences all around the world. So long as anyone watches the show two nights in succession, the intrinsic conflict built into the show is overwhelming. What more basic, anatomical conflict between humans can there be but that between male and female, yet how dependent each is on the other? The premise is established unequivocally right from the start. And so it easily leads to the conflict of another kind, between good and evil, captor and criminal.

It is a simple logic of the show's premise, therefore, that the moderator, she or he, conflicted with him- or her-self, sits at the centre of the table, flanked on one side by the captor and the other side by the criminal.

Now that we have provided the *raison d'être* of the show we may continue to the edited highlights of the very first show that broke all records for a pilot show. It was a Monday show, so Tommie was dressed as a female as we have already described. The guest felon was a serial murderer and rapist who, as the media promoted and we were happy to confirm, made Hannibal the cannibal seem pretty tame, and as well was way smarter than was Hannibal (who was a fictitious character anyway). This guy was real. (We use the past tense because he was killed under suspicious circumstances when he escaped from the Pope-mobile look alike and was run down by a hit and run driver, an old guy driving a vintage K-car, according to witnesses.) The following is an abridged version of the original transcript, reproduced using the exact script format.

Series 1: The Tommie Felon Show
Episode 1. The Sado-Rapist

Directed by Quince Titillatio
Produced by Ozone TV in collaboration with
the Felony Foundation
*The advice and assistance of the society of felons is gratefully
acknowledged*

TOMMIE prances on to the set and advances to the front of the stage. She wears a bright, iridescent green cloak that she hugs with both arms across her bosom. With a wonderful flourish, she opens the cloak and stands tall, her arms extended up, holding her cloak as though she were Batman. She flings the cloak to the audience, and there are squeals and screams as those in the front seat fight to claim it. Her cloaks, made of recycled and sustainable tissue and coloured with the slime of the slugs who inhabit the Olympic Peninsula, have become a valued collector's item. She blows kisses to the audience, steps down to the front few rows and kisses her fingers, then touches them on the heads of worshipping admirers. She returns to the stage, her back to the audience, then suddenly swivels around, her head buried in her hands, lily-white elbows pointing to the floor. It is the cue for the audience to go quiet. She raises her head slowly from her hands, her face showing pain, her eyes tearing, painted eyebrows slanting inwards.

TOMMIE

Oh, my Dears! What a show we have for you tonight! An evil thoroughly despicable killer and rapist who has done terrible things to his victims, things that even you, my dears, could not imagine!

AUDIENCE
(chanting)
Tommie dearest! Tommie dearest!

TOMMIE

Yes, my dears. I do this for you! Only you! But can you bear it? Do you really want him? He is so terrible, so frightening, so horrible!

AUDIENCE
Bring him on! Bring him on!

TOMMIE

Then I present to you, our felon of the day, killer, rapist and vivisector, a man whose name we refuse to speak, the felon himself!

A security guard drags the criminal on stage, as he staggers under his chains that clank loudly nearly pulling him to the floor. CRIMINAL swears at his attendants and makes obscene gestures at the audience to the extent that his chains allow. The guard roughly pushes CRIMINAL forward and on to the chair. TOMMIE prances to the CRIMINAL and gracefully places herself on his lap, leans back, kicking her leg closest to the audience out in a wonderful ballet pose. CRIMINAL tries to grope her bosom, snarls, and drools, but TOMMIE quickly slides off and takes her seat at the table, sitting up straight and formal. She speaks directly into the TV camera.

TOMMIE

And now I present to you our felon's accuser, tormentor, or is he also his excuser?

TOMMIE looks slyly at the audience.

                          AUDIENCE
                          (chanting)
Scuser! Scuser! Scuser!
                          TOMMIE
Yes, yes, yes! I present to you our world famous
excuser of criminals, Dr. Fallatious Hood, the greatest
Hoodie I know!
                          AUDIENCE
                          (chanting)
Hood-EE! Hood-EE!

HOOD, the accuser, and tormentor, a lofty forensic psychiatrist,
quietly slips on to the set, seeming to appear from behind our
transgendered moderator. TOMMIE extends her hand briefly to
HOOD but retrieves it quickly after their eyes meet for an instant. She
immediately turns to the CRIMINAL, licks her bright red lips in a
tantalizing manner, and grasps his chained hand tightly in hers. She
stands and raises the CRIMINAL'S hand with hers.
                          TOMMIE
My dear friends. I present to you, on my left, evil!
                          AUDIENCE
Eee-vil! Eee-vil!

CRIMINAL scowls right on cue. TOMMIE stretches for HOOD's
hand and raises it too.
                          TOMMIE
My dear friends. I present to you, on my right, good!
                          AUDIENCE
Boo-oo, good! Boo-oo good!

HOOD pulls his hand away and leans forward, staring into criminal's
eyes.
                          TOMMIE
Dr. Hood. You first. The good must lead the way!
Ask the question that everyone wants to be
answered!
                          HOOD
That's easy. Everyone wants to know why you do it.
                          CRIMINAL
Do what?

                    HOOD
Don't play cute with me, you filthy scum. Vicious,
sadistic rape and murder of course.
                    TOMMIE
Doctor! Doctor! Tut! Tut!
                    AUDIENCE
Tut! Tut! -- Tut! Tut!
                    CRIMINAL
I enjoy it, that's why I do it. I would have thought it
was obvious.
                    HOOD

Enjoy?

TOMMIE sighs and looks bored. She puts on her headset and sways
rhythmically as she listens to Iz Mer, Turkish rap star, currently her
favourite.

                    CRIMINAL
Yes, rape and killing. It's very pleasurable.
                    HOOD
Pleasurable?

TOMMIE rolls her eyes and signals to the audience to don their
headsets.

                    CRIMINAL
Well, no—more than that!
                    HOOD
How many have you—?
                    CRIMINAL
Oh! Who can say? There's been so many—
                    HOOD
And what methods do you use?

TOMMIE removes her headset and leans over to CRIMINAL,
beckons to audience
                    TOMMIE
Oooooooh! Aaaaaah!!

AUDIENCE
Oooooh! Aaaaah!
CRIMINAL
Well, I prefer to use instruments that happen to be around at the time. A kind of situational ethics, if you see what I mean. There's a symmetry about it. Strangle her with her own stocking, put out her eyes with her own lip-stick case. Or shoes—shoes are really good. You can do a lot with shoes—

CRIMINAL'S voice trails away.

HOOD
Anything else?
CRIMINAL
Well, I couldn't describe them all. Take too long. I suppose you'd say it's the blood that's the best part.
AUDIENCE
(Conducted by Tommie)
Tell us! (clapping) Tell us! (clapping)
HOOD
And, er—the other part?
CRIMINAL
You mean rape?
AUDIENCE
Ooooh!

TOMMIE puts her hand to her ear, leans over to the criminal.

HOOD
Ahem, er, yes.
CRIMINAL
Of course, that's a good part of it too. I couldn't describe them all.
HOOD
Well, just some of the better ones—
CRIMINAL
The better ones you wouldn't exactly define as er—
HOOD
What do you mean?

                    CRIMINAL
        Well, because I don't do it in the er—

                    HOOD
        Oh, you mean anal intercourse?

TOMMIE rolls her eyes, dons headset

                    CRIMINAL
        Oh no! That's nothing!
                    HOOD
        Then?
                    CRIMINAL
        No, well, I —
TOMMIE removes headset, beckons audience.
                    HOOD
        Go on.
                    CRIMINAL
        No, I'm not going there. Let's just say that I do what-
        ever I must to maximize my pleasure.

TOMMIE jumps up from her seat and runs to the front of the table.
She conducts the audience in exaggerated gestures.
                    AUDIENCE
                (chants, clapping)
        Tell us! Tell us! Tell us!
                    CRIMINAL
                (flattered by audience attention)
        Have you ever read American Psycho?
                    HOOD
        I wouldn't waste my time with such trash.
                    TOMMIE
                (chanting)
        Yes, we have! Yes, we have!

TOMMIE rushes to the front of the stage, waving her arms.

                    AUDIENCE
                (chanting)
        Yes, we have! Yes, we have!

CRIMINAL

Then you're ignorant. I've gone well beyond that smart ass from the Hamptons. Drills, saws, rats. I've done way better than that.

HOOD leans forward, aggressively, stares at CRIMINAL

HOOD

Why do you do it?

CRIMINAL

I just answered that, didn't I?

HOOD

Not really.

CRIMINAL

What do you mean, then?

HOOD

The killing and the rape, why?

TOMMIE waves to the audience again.

TOMMIE AND AUDIENCE
(chanting)

Bor-ing! Bor-ing!

CRIMINAL

I remember there was one time when I felt I would never find one to satisfy me. I'd just finished my finals and was watching a football game in a run-down bar. This raunchiness hit me. I just had to find the hottest, roughest one—

TOMMIE rushes back to her seat, and with an exaggerated flourish sits and leans over to the criminal, hand to ear

HOOD

But why?

CRIMINAL

Why what? I just told you, didn't I?

HOOD

Why kill them?

CRIMINAL
Before or after?

HOOD leans back, exasperated. TOMMIE pivots to him and gives him an exaggerated hug, and looks deep into the camera.

TOMMIE
My poor dear! It must be so hard for you.
AUDIENCE
(sighs and swoons).
HOOD
Either.
CRIMINAL
Well, I mean they're not much use afterward, are they? Besides, they might remember what I looked like.

HOOD
Aha! So you're afraid of being caught!
CRIMINAL
Well of course! Wouldn't anyone?

TOMMIE leaps up and runs to the front, laughing hysterically, the audience joins in.

HOOD
But you're not just anyone--
CRIMINAL
What do you mean?

TOMMIE returns to her seat and with her chin in her chest, croons to the camera
TOMMIE
Oooh! Dark! Oooh, spooky!
AUDIENCE
Spooooky!
HOOD
Well, you're different.
CRIMINAL
What?

                    HOOD
Different. You know. I mean not everyone goes
around killing and raping.
                  CRIMINAL
Yes, the pathetic fools! If only they could!
                    HOOD
Anyway, let's get back to it. Why are you frightened
of getting caught?
                  CRIMINAL
That's a really stupid question—
                  AUDIENCE
Stu-pid! Stu-pid!
                  CRIMINAL
As I said before, who wouldn't be?
                    HOOD
But you keep doing it, you must have realized you'd
get caught sooner or later. Surely—
                  CRIMINAL
So?

                   TOMMIE
          (leaning into HOOD'S face)
Yes, so?
                    HOOD
So, why keep doing it?
                  CRIMINAL
Because it makes life bearable if I assume I'll never
be caught.

                    HOOD
But you have been!
                  CRIMINAL
So that's life. You've probably got terminal cancer.

CRIMINAL chuckles, looks to audience for approval. TOMMIE
laughs raucously. Audience joins in.
                    HOOD
                (very serious)
We're going round in circles.

TOMMIE puts her finger to her lips and raises her hand to the audience. Silence ensues.

> HOOD
>
> Let me start again. Why do you kill people?

> CRIMINAL
>
> I just do it. It's who I am. It's my life. I love my life. Who doesn't?

> HOOD
>
> Don't you care for other people?

> TOMMIE AND AUDIENCE
> (chanting)
>
> Doesn't care! Doesn't care!

> CRIMINAL
> (outraged)
>
> What?

> HOOD
>
> I said, don't you care for other people?

> CRIMINAL
>
> Of course, I do. What sort of a question is that supposed to be?

> HOOD
>
> Then why do you do it?

> CRIMINAL
>
> What?

> HOOD
>
> Why? Why?

HOOD leans across the table and grabs the criminal by the throat.

> AUDIENCE
> (chanting)
>
> Why! Why!

CRIMINAL tries to push back but his chains will not let him. TOMMIE stands back, hands on hips.

> TOMMIE
>
> Go Doc! Go Doc!

> AUDIENCE
>
> Go doc! Go doc!

                    HOOD
Tell me! Tell me!
                  CRIMINAL
You're hurting me!

CRIMINAL stands pulling his restraining chains tight, catching
TOMMIE'S extended arm, ensnaring HOOD'S hand as well. They
all struggle and fall in a heap behind the table.
                   TOMMIE
Oh, Doctor! Oh, Doctor! Save me!

TOMMIE flings herself back, legs flying up in a classic V position,
kicking the table over. Members of the audience run up to save her,
but they are restrained by security guards.

                    HOOD
Oh! Sorry! I, I didn't mean to—
                  CRIMINAL
That's what they all say.

TOMMIE crawls, half drags herself to the front of the stage. Her
contortions are Shakespearian.
                   TOMMIE
Oh my dear, dear friends! I thank you with all my
heart. Why does the doctor behave so badly?
                HOOD (contrite)
All I asked was why he does it.

HOOD stands as if to leave.
                  CRIMINAL
You must know why. You're the psychiatrist after all
                    HOOD
               (glaring at Tommie)
You are a despicable, evil person—
                TOMMIE (shocked)
Who, me?

TOMMIE points at her breast with both hands. She looks at the
audience seeking approval.

                    AUDIENCE
    Yes, you! Yes, You!

TOMMIE feigns horror, runs to the doctor and hugs him

                     TOMMIE
    Please stay doctor. We all need you! You're the only
    doctor we have!
                      HOOD
    There doesn't seem to be much point in continuing
    this interview.

CRIMINAL untangles his chains and gets back to his seat.

                    CRIMINAL
    Oh! But I thought you wanted to find out all about
    my crimes?
                      HOOD
    I did—I do!
                     TOMMIE
    Oh, thank you, doctor! Thank you!

TOMMIE kisses the psychiatrist full on the lips then waltzes down to
the front row of the audience and brings up an overweight man in his
thirties to help right the table. TOMMIE kisses him too, on the cheek,
then dismisses him to the care of a security guard.

                    CRIMINAL
    All right then, ask me some questions.
                      HOOD
    I have, and you won't answer them.
                    CRIMINAL
    You haven't given me a chance.
                      HOOD
    I've pleaded with you.
                    CRIMINAL
    I've tried to answer you, honestly.
                      HOOD
                   (despondent)
    It's no use.

                        TOMMIE
There, there Doctor. I'm sure he doesn't mean it, do
you Mr. Criminal?
                        AUDIENCE
                        (chanting)
Mean it! Mean it!
                        CRIMINAL
Why don't you ask me about my childhood? Every-
body else does.
                        HOOD
                        (fed up).
All right then. What about your childhood?
                        CRIMINAL
Well, I mean, you'll have to be a bit more specific.
                        HOOD
                        (disinterested).
Yes, I suppose so. You were an illegitimate, only
child, I suppose?
                        CRIMINAL
No, certainly not. I have two elder brothers and two
younger sisters. Our family is very close.
                        HOOD
Your father left home when you were five or six,
having beaten you mercilessly since birth?
                        CRIMINAL
No! Good heavens, you must have had a terrible
childhood!

TOMMIE stands, signals to the audience, and conducts as if they
were a choir.
                    TOMMIE AND AUDIENCE
The doctor was abused! The doctor was abused!
                        HOOD
Well, it wasn't the happiest, but—
                        CRIMINAL
Were you close to your parents? I was. All us kids
were. We were a very close family. Loved each other.
The usual arguments occasionally, but generally a
wonderful family.

> HOOD
> (slyly)

And your mother. Why haven't you mentioned your mother?

> CRIMINAL

You didn't ask me. Besides, it's implied when I say 'family.'

> HOOD

You mean your mother was nothing special?

> CRIMINAL

That's not what I said!

HOOD writes down notes.

> HOOD

I see.

> CRIMINAL

Are you really taking that down?

> HOOD

Of course.

> CRIMINAL

But you've invented it. That's not what I said at all. That's dishonest.

> HOOD

Nonsense! Now let's get on with the questions. Your mother—

> CRIMINAL

You can't justify it. You're dishonest.

> HOOD

Your mother—

CRIMINAL jumps up, one of the chains pulling free. A security guard rushes forward to restrain him.

> CRIMINAL

You're nothing but a faker, a quack!

TOMMIE'S eyes light up. She signals to the audience once more, though it needs no asking.

> AUDIENCE

Quack! Quack!

HOOD

It's not dishonest. It's a matter of interpretation. I've studied criminals for years. It's my expert opinion.

CRIMINAL

Expert dishonesty.
HOOD

I'm a very experienced forensic psychiatrist. I make careful scientific impartial judgments.
AUDIENCE

Lies! Lies! — Lies! Lies!

CRIMINAL looks to the audience with approval. Blows them a kiss, but gets an unexpected response.

AUDIENCE

Kill the quack! Kill the quack!
CRIMINAL
(enraged)
Barbarians! I don't kill just anyone!!
TOMMIE

Now! Now! Mr. Criminal. Remember, they will vote for your release as will our viewers!
CRIMINAL

Where's the pleasure in killing the quack? Now if they wanted me to kill you—
HOOD

Mr. Felon! Look Out!
TOMMIE

It's not Mister, and you know it, you insensitive brute!
HOOD

Miss, Mrs., then. Whatever. You're in danger! Get away quickly!
TOMMIE

It's Madam, if you don't mind!
AUDIENCE

Look out! Look out! Madam, look out!

CRIMINAL wrenches himself up off his seat and thrusts his body and chains with all his might towards TOMMIE who puts both hands to her throat and tries to slide under the table out of the way. HOOD pushes his chair back, watches, and takes notes.

TOMMIE
Help me! Help me, my God help me!

Security guards rush forward, but it's too late. CRIMINAL slipped under the table and has wrapped Tommie in his chains. He bites off her ear lobe and spits it out at the audience.

CRIMINAL
Fellow barbarians! I give you blood!
AUDIENCE
Blood! Blood! He gave us blood!

HOOD scurries off the set, walking backward, half bent over and hoping not to be noticed. TOMMIE swoons and licks her own blood as it trickles down her face. CRIMINAL follows her example and licks the blood off her cheek.

TOMMIE
Oh! Mr. Criminal! Why me? Why me?

TOMMIE becomes listless and floppy, as though in a drunken stupor. CRIMINAL looks out at the audience.

CRIMINAL
Neck or nose? Neck or nose?
AUDIENCE
Neck! Neck! — Neck! Neck!

CRIMINAL bares his teeth like a snarling dog. But a young security guard, pretending to participate in the blood-licking, has crawled under the table and, after one lick, lifts a leg and fiercely rams it into CRIMINAL'S chin, causing him to bite off his own tongue. The guard unravels the chains from TOMMIE and pulls her free. She envelops him in her not so floppy arms and guides him to the front of the stage as they stagger together. There is blood on both their faces. The audience stands and jumps and screams in ecstasy.

AUDIENCE
Kiss! Kiss!—Kiss! Kiss!

As the ecstatic couple complies all too well with the audience demands, other guards have not managed to unravel CRIMINAL'S chains from the table and chairs, so they drag him off the set along with the table and a chair. CRIMINAL gasps, chokes, face turning blue, blood pours from his mouth. TOMMIE and the security guard come out of their embrace. Tommie swoons again and waves to the audience.

TOMMIE
My dears! My dears! You have saved me! I owe you
my love and my life!

TOMMIE falls back into the security guard's arms.

TOMMIE (CONT.)
Take me! Take me!

Security guard lifts TOMMIE off her feet and carries her off the set while she blows kisses to the audience.

And there we have it. This was the most highly rated season premiere ever of a talk show (to repeat, repetition is good in our business). For your curiosity, the studio audience voted to parole the criminal immediately, but the viewing audience did not agree. It voted overwhelmingly for a continued sentence of life in prison without parole, with a sizable portion of respondents urging that the original death sentence, which was commuted by then Governor Bunyon, be restored. (As an aside, a sizable minority also urged that the psychiatrist's license be revoked).

Please be aware that Tommie is well and her ear lobe has been reattached successfully. However, the security guard was fired for the liberties he took in saving her, specifically licking the blood from her face, which, the gender harassment board in its review, rated as an unnecessary invasion of Tommie's privacy and was, in fact, a sexually tinged touching. As for the criminal, the prison surgeon was unable to reattach the pieces of his tongue since it seems that he chewed them up thinking that they were pieces of Tommie's ear. In fact, the surgeon had to remove additional parts of the tongue because of the danger that rough edges in the mouth may turn cancerous. The criminal launched proceedings against Ozone TV claiming several million dollars in damages, but the judge threw out the case because (1) the damage was self-inflicted and (2) the contract the criminal signed with Ozone TV clearly specified that we would not be held liable for any damages that resulted from the criminal's actions. Clearly, all the unfortunate spilling of blood was his doing, not ours. His lawyer claimed that we should have foreseen the events and chained the criminal down more securely, but our consideration, in this case, was that we did not want to treat the criminal in an inhumane manner. As it was, we received a considerable amount of mail from viewers, and media pundits that we had, in fact, weighed the criminal down with so many chains that he was treated like a beast of burden. The criminal has appealed the case to the U.S. district court, but we are confident that the court will not hear the case.

Clearly, we are breaking new ground with this show. This is real time television, in no way edited or scripted. In fact, as can be seen from this "ad hoc" script that if one were to actually write such a script and expect players to act (no, be) the part, we could not write in the actual spilling of blood as occurred in this episode. Of course, we could have people act the parts out and have special effects make the spilling of blood seem real, but that is not our idea of reality TV. There is no script. We do create an environment with participants we have carefully chosen, and we do, of course, employ a moderator who is incredibly talented. Tommie's behaviour we can more or less predict, and the same goes for the audience. However, we cannot predict precisely what the guests will do. This is what makes The Tommie Felon Show so exciting and why people all over the world tune into it with high expectations that we try not to disappoint.

We are confident that the proposed franchise of the show to the new and exciting Lor-Renz Arabia TV network will be equally successful. We are working with them right now to develop the set, which will be based on the notorious Abu Ghraib prison, in fact, may even be shot on site (pun intended!). Guests will include high ranking Al Qaeda or ISIS operatives, one in particular who has perfected the skill of beheading hostages, and others including dedicated suicide bombers of various sizes and ages and genders, and on the contra side, prosecutors and interrogators who have perfected the procedures for extracting the truth from their quarry, including the efficient means of punishment for the convicted such as beheading and cutting off other limbs with one stroke of the sword, and the use of hot water boarding.

Speaking of which, we have engaged the services of a well-known Hollywood head hunting team to find the very best moderator for the show. Naturally, we are not looking for a transgendered person, but rather for a terrorist with a strong history of violence who is also a doctor and pacifist, thus providing the standard premise of the show: a balance between prosecutors and defenders, violence and peace, good and evil.

3. Easter Story

The price of lamb is priceless

When I was about six years old, my father came home from the fields with a great surprise. He trudged down the dusty road, his baggy trousers tied up with an old piece of string and stained all down the front. We had a kind of unwritten agreement about how things should proceed. I squatted down in the middle of the road, staring into the distance, watching my papa gradually grow from a dark speck in the fields of olives to the big, awkward figure that I loved. We pretended not to see each other until he came within about twenty paces. Then I darted forward, like a sprinter, calling out, "Papa! Papa!" and launched myself into the air, aiming directly for his breast.

He dropped the old canvas sack in which he carried his bread and wine, and, hugging me tightly, whizzed me around several times.

Holding me at arm's length, he cried, "ma come sei bellina" and pinched each of my cheeks.

I hung on one of his arms, rubbing the back of his hand against my face, and said, "did you work hard today papa?"

And he replied, "si, si, molto, molto, and how about you?"

"Oh, very hard papa," I said with a grin.

By this time the sun had dropped just below the horizon, plunging into darkness the two narrow cross-streets and four winding alleys of our village, which now glowed like the Forbidden City. Our house stood at the edge of the village in one of the newer cement and stucco apartment buildings, and as we reached it, papa always stopped and looked towards the dim outline of our small church, which had been restored from its medieval ruins with patches of iron and cement. I too stopped, then followed him inside our house where my mother, having toiled all day, raised her head from the old stove and smiled at my father, who seemed barely to notice.

"It's ready, it's ready," mamma said. Papa sat at the table, let me climb on his lap, and we ate our supper together. When he had filled up with pasta and mopped up the sparse sauce with big chunks of bread, I slid off his knee and looked up at him expectantly. We usually played a game, or he told me a story of some other village, or of an incident that had happened in the fields where he worked each day.

On this evening, papa grinned at me, the old hairs in his rose bristling like a cat's, and said, "I have a big surprise for you, my carina."

"Where is it papa, where is it?" I called excitedly, jumping up and down.

"Well, it's not here yet, but it should be here any time now. A friend I work with in the fields is bringing it in his old truck."

"Ooh: What is it papa, what is it?"

"You'll see, you'll see," he replied as he carried me under his arm, out the door, and into the dark street.

Softly, we sang a few songs together, and I pranced up and down before him, throwing my spindly legs loosely around, in the way that pleased papa very much. He leaned up against the stucco wall, a loosely rolled cigarette dangling from his lip, chuckling at my antics, occasionally clapping in time with my steps. Then he stopped in the middle of a clap.

"Sh! Listen! Do you hear it?"

"What, papa?"

"The old truck. Your surprise is coming."

"Ooh: Papa!" I ran and hugged him tightly, my curly locks catching in his shirt buttons. We walked out into the centre of the rocky road and squinted together. The lights of the truck were just discernible in the half light of early evening, and we waited silently, watching, listening to the groan of its engine grow louder and louder. When the truck entered the edge of the village, we ran to the side of the road, waving and calling out.

"Sandro!" called my father, "you're always on time!"

"Si, si, I have much to do this time of the year."

He jumped down from the old truck, and only then did I hear the frantic bleating of the lambs that were loaded on the back.

"Which one do you want?" Sandro asked as he looked to my father and then to me.

Papa hugged me close and said, "The one with the best meat, of course." He laughed lightly.

I laughed too and repeated, "yes, the best meat," but then proceeded to choose the prettiest and smallest with little tufts of wool sticking out from the base of its ears, a lively look to its eyes, and a floppy tail that it seemed barely able to swish.

Sandro looked to my father who shrugged and nodded his head. I stretched out my arms and lovingly received my surprise, a bundle of cuddly wool and four undisciplined legs. I immediately named him (actually I discovered later it was a her, but that didn't matter) Little Gesu, because it was only two weeks to Easter.

The next thirteen days were like a dream. I tormented my mother until she rummaged through her old chest and found a baby's teat, which I attached to a bottle and used to feed my little Gesu milk every morning (when there was any over) and water as often as I could. He was very easy to train, so we started to go for walks the second day, and I taught him to stay close to my heel, not to wander in the long grass, to stop and nibble the dry grass only when I permitted. Of course, he was so young and full of fun, that he disobeyed my commands often so I would chase him over the hard ground, and he would struggle happily over mounds, his splayed legs sometimes giving way to his body. I would catch him, hold his head in my hands and speak to him saying, "You naughty little fellow," and I swear his eyes would light up, and his face actually smile. We learned to roll in the grass, he licked my face, and I kissed him, and we did many other tricks together.

Each evening we waited in the middle of the road for papa to return from the fields, and papa would lift us both up and hug us, always with the question, "have you fed him well? You have not run the fat off him, I hope?"

"Oh no, papa."

Each night, we left Gesu tethered to a little pole outside our house while we went in for supper. Mother always cooked an especially nutritious bread for Little Gesu which papa and I fed him as soon as we had finished our meal. When I went to bed, I worried about him being left alone in the kitchen. "He is only a baby after all, and babies should never be left alone," I pleaded to mamma, in an effort to be allowed to take him into bed with me.

The thirteenth day, the day before Good Friday, came so very quickly. I now talked to my little surprise as though he were an old friend. We knew each other very well. On that morning, I fed him his bottle, as usual, before I went off to school. I pleaded to be allowed to stay home with him for his last day, but mamma would have none of it. I tried throwing a tantrum, feigning illness, even managing to vomit up my breakfast, but to no avail. I cruelly claimed that if papa were there (he had left for the fields hours before), he would let me.

And this, of course, made mamma even angrier and more resolute. As a last resort, I encouraged little Gesu to follow me to school, so mamma locked him in the toilet, such as it was, until I went.

I remember nothing of school that day. The pages and pencils were a blur, the teacher's voice an irrelevant buzz. As soon as the bell went, I rushed home, running the mile or so without a stop, falling down when I reached him, too exhausted to hug him or to speak. He went down on his forelegs, and burrowed his nose into my arm pit, invoking an exquisite sensation of love in me which I carry to this day.

My father always came home a few hours early the day before Good Friday. We were waiting for him at our usual place on the road, a strong breeze hurling handfuls of dust into our faces. Little Gesu did not falter one step and showed no signs of nervousness. As soon as we had gone through our rituals with papa, he placed his sack in the kitchen and came out with a large kitchen knife which he loudly sharpened before our eyes. Gesu looked on trustingly, with an expectant calm, for he understood exactly what was to happen and why it must be so. But I must admit to an uneasy feeling of apprehension, anxiety, or perhaps the better word is awe, even though I had witnessed my father slaughter the Easter lamb in every year of my childhood.

The sun caught the edge of the knife and sent a dart of fire into my eyes. I squinted, and they watered a little. Papa stopped sharpening the knife.

"Hold his head back so I can get a clear swipe at his throat, carina," he said lovingly.

This was the first time he had ever asked me to help in this distasteful task. I felt flattered. I held back the head, Gesu's little-tufted ears sticking through my fingers.

"Va bene, papa?" I asked, trying to be very businesslike.

"Si, si. Molto bene."

With a smooth stroke, papa drew the knife across Gesu's throat, and the blood poured out into the old saucepan papa had placed below. Mamma would make a delicious chocolate spread with that. My little surprise gave only a few tiny kicks with his spindly legs, and I watched his eyes gradually gloss over as his life dripped away into the saucepan. Papa trussed his back legs together, then hung the carcass on a hook that he had driven into the wall of our house.

Suddenly I felt terribly hungry and dirty. I ran in to wash my hands, then sat down to a mighty plate of spaghetti which mamma always had waiting. But after the first couple of mouthfuls, I felt so full inside, I could eat no more. I pushed the plate away and mamma, on cue, cried, "mangia!" I felt so full I could burst, and when mamma picked up the spoon ready to feed me herself, the howls that came from deep in my heart spurted out of my ears, my eyes, my mouth, my head, like the water of a fountain. I lashed out at the spoon, knocking it onto the tiled floor. Mamma was angry.

"You killed my baby: You killed my baby!" I cried, and ran to my bed, delicately sidestepping my mother's attempt to slap my face. She called out something about my being ungrateful, and that I'd change my mind when it came to eating it since tomorrow was a day of fasting. I sobbed well into the night.

After my mother had cooled down, she came over to my bed and hugged me so tightly it hurt. She tried to explain to me that it was because Gesu loved us that we killed the lamb. Or was it because we loved the lamb that we killed it? I was bewildered, and still can't remember exactly what she said. Papa remained silent. He just came after mamma and held me lightly against his smelly old chest, rocking me back and forth as I sobbed.

I never ate the Easter lamb, and I kept on sobbing for many days. Mamma plied me with all manner of brews and potions, but I remained a pathetic little creature who burst into tears at the slightest provocation.

I still waited on the road each evening for my father to return from the fields, but I no longer leaped into his arms. There were no more songs or games. He told me stories, but I wept too often because I saw sadness in even the happiest stories.

One evening when I lay sobbing myself to sleep, mamma and papa came to my bed, sat on each side of me, holding hands across my little body, a look of tenderness in both their eyes that I had never seen before.

"We have a surprise for you," whispered my mother in a very proud way.

My sobbing stopped instantly. Could it be? Another lamb so soon to replace my little Gesu? Surely it was not Easter already? I sat up, wide-eyed, smiling, the tears dried up.

"Where? What is it? May I see it?"

"Well, it's not that kind of a surprise—at least not yet," said my mother mysteriously.

"Mamma! Tell me, tell me!"

"Tell the girl," said papa impatiently, but also with pride.

"You see how big my belly has become?"

"Yes, I see." It seemed an utterly irrelevant question. "What surprise mamma?"

Mamma straightened up a little. "Well, I'm going to have a little baby, a little brother or sister for you. Isn't that the best surprise there is?"

Mamma and papa smiled so innocently, obviously expecting a rapturous response. I was shocked.

"Well, what do you say?" asked mamma, sensing my lack of enthusiasm.

"Oh, how lovely!" I lied, "I'll have my own little surprise."

Mamma was satisfied. She leaned over to kiss my forehead, then her mouth broke into a smile big enough to blot out her haggard features. She lifted my hands and pressed them to her lips. Papa gave me a rough jostle, and I giggled.

Then I was left alone in my bed. I turned over on my belly and pressed my cheek against the pillow, which was still damp from my tears. I thought some more about how I missed little Gesu, and my tears almost welled up again. But I forced myself to be a grateful child, and tried to smile at the thought of Gesu's little replacement, sure it would be a baby brother, I would name him Gesu, or perhaps "Agnelletto," and I could feed and train my little brother just as I did the lamb. A fitful sleep overtook me. And when I awoke, I no longer cried. But it took a lot to make me happy.

Then Angelo was born. And when mamma and papa brought him home, I tried to be happy. They let me hold him, and I did, though I did not want to. I was scared I might drop him for one thing. But I also didn't love him like I did little Gesu, even though mamma had let me name him Angelo.

As I grew older along with Angelo, I started to stay in my bed more and more. In the mornings I didn't want to wake up, and mamma called me in her loud voice. She thought I didn't want to go to school, but it wasn't that. It was just that when I had little Gesu, I woke up each morning, very early in the mornings, with such joy and happiness looking forward to the day, playing with him, teaching him tricks, hugging him and holding his twisting body in my arms.

With Angelo, there was nothing like that to look forward to. Mamma had taken to nagging at me to get out of bed, complaining that I was making life hard for her now that she had Angelo to feed. He was a little baby that needed all her attention, and if I was a good girl, I would get out of bed and help her. At last, I would get out of bed, and I would help her, even give Angelo his bottle when mamma ran out of milk. I tried, I really tried, to think of my feeding Angelo like I was feeding little Gesu. But Angelo's squirming and spitting up wasn't cute and funny, not like Gesu when he tugged so furiously at the bottle and he looked at me with those pure, innocent eyes, and the tufts of wool around his neck tickled my arm. Instead, Angelo was a nuisance.

What got me out of bed wasn't mamma's nagging. I started to dream about playing with Angelo. I planned to dress him up like a little lamb and teach him tricks like I did Gesu. The trouble was that this was such a lovely dream that I didn't want it to end, so sometimes I would be so deeply asleep my mamma had to shake me to wake me up.

At last, Angelo was big enough to crawl around and then to walk. I had waited so long for this. I pestered mamma to buy me some lamb's wool and to teach me how to knit. She was so relieved to see me come out of my funk that she scrounged up the money and we went to the village to buy some wool. In no time I had knitted Angelo a little sweater, and mamma helped me sew on it a little lamb's tail and a little lamb's face on the front.

"When Angelo wakes up from his nap you can put it on him if you like, carina," she said happily.

"Can I?" I cried clapping my hands. It was like I had little Gesu all over again.

I sat drawing at the kitchen table, waiting for my little brother to wake. Mamma patted my head and said, "is that little Gesu or little Angelo?"

I had drawn several figures in poses that I thought were happy, jumping and dancing in the fields. And there were lots of flowers, I remember that. I had not seriously thought to myself who or what these figures represent. I must have been about six or seven years old. I'm really not sure. So when my mamma asked me who they were I at first didn't answer.

"Carina?" she pressed, "are they Angelo and Gesu?"

With an unsteady finger, I finally pointed to one figure and said it was Gesu, then to another and said it was Angelo. But I hadn't made up my mind, and I resented being forced to distinguish between them.

"Oh that's lovely, dear," mamma said, "it's so lovely, and papa will be so happy that you've drawn such a beautiful picture."

At last, we heard Angelo's cry from the next room. He was awake at last! I followed my mamma into the room and watched her gently lift Angelo out of his crib and change his diaper. This naked little boy without fur. How could he compare to my little Gesu?

Angelo kicked and screamed. He didn't like being changed, especially just when he woke up. Mamma hugged him to her and rocked him, and at last, he calmed down. I held the little lamb's sweater up for mamma to put on him. We went out into the kitchen, and she sat on a chair and stood Angelo on the floor. He smiled and made a cooing sound. I held out the little sweater again, and mamma took it. She asked me to hold Angelo while she pulled open the sweater and began to slide it over his head and push his arms through the sleeves. Angelo hated it. He screamed and pushed it away. He flailed his arms around, so it was impossible for mamma to get it on him. I let go of him, horrified. This was not my dream. This was a nightmare. I ran to my room crying out as I went, "I hate him! I hate him!"

Mamma did not come to me. She was busy calming Angelo. I sobbed into my pillow, and it was like Gesu had been killed all over again.

That's really the end of the story. I'm grown up now, and so is Angelo. I'm not planning to marry, least of all have children. I rarely see Angelo, in fact, I try not to. It's not that I don't love him and all that. It's just that every time I see him, a flood of tears wells up inside me and I feel so silly. That wouldn't be so bad except that for weeks, even months after I see him, I start dreaming again. It's a dream no one would want to have, and I can't get rid of it. I see my papa holding back the head of little Gesu and cutting his throat. And he hangs him upside down on the old hook and, well, you can guess what happens next. The lamb turns into Angelo.

4. Veggies

In beans we trust

Four children at play
Selling vegetables.
An icebox filled with beans
Beside a dusty road.
Out of the dust a white truck.
Children jump and wave.
"Got tomatoes?"
Heads shake.
She offers beans
The truck door opens.
He takes her hand.
The beans fall.
Now there are three.

5. Wombattered

A car and a wombat meet

Four legs point up
From a furry balloon,
Laid back ears hidden
Its growl unheard
Why not roll over?
The force of rubber,
The force of metal,
On wheels.

6. Death at the Y

It's not Venice but it might as well be

Thomas carefully folded his small super fibre towel and wiped off the remaining smudge of moisture left on the seat of the weight machine. It was one of those where you sit leaning back, legs open, and push up against mechanical arms. He had turned to face the machine when he saw out of the corner of his eye his wife of 42 years already beckoning to him to hurry on. She was heading for the tread mill, her one machine. She waddled forward, overweight, loose jowls of flesh swinging from her upper arms, a rear end big enough to stop a bus. If she fell or sat on him, he would disappear as though under a massive rubber ball. That's why he always kept his distance from her when they came to the Y or went walking, always ten feet behind. A mark of respect or submission, he supposed people thought, but actually it amounted to self-preservation. There were three more machines left in his routine. He'd do them slowly as he always did, timed to finish exactly when she stepped off the treadmill.

It was Monday. The big clock above the row of TV screens showed 9.45 am. He followed her down the stairs to the locker rooms. She to hers, he, passing the door marked BOYS UNDER 16 ONLY to the one marked MEN. His locker was the one in the far corner. He would undo the combination lock, rummage for his shower stuff, undress, walk across to the showers, fiddle with the leaking shower faucets, vigorously dry off, then step on the scales and issue a silent grunt of satisfaction when everything looked the same. Thomas repeated this routine every day except the weekend when they went shopping at the mall and had lunch at the retro diner. But this morning was different. It was because of what he had seen or thought he had seen, up in the weight room. When he had sat back down on his machine and squinted across the room, a bead of sweat sliding into his eye clouding his vision, he saw the fuzzy image of a young beauty, partially hidden by his wife's rump. He had blinked and wiped his eyes but saw no beauty. The girl was gone, but the fuzzy image, more and more beautiful, remained. He went through his routine in the locker room this Monday morning, as in a trance.

On Tuesday morning he was ready earlier than usual, impatient to get to the gym. She struggled to get into the back seat of the car, wrapped as she was in her puffy goose down coat, so he gave her a bit of a push and very soon he was following her up the stairs to the weight room. He logged in to his machines and walked to his first station, scanning the entire room for the confirmation of his beautiful image. He saw only his wife. The morning's workout went incredibly slowly. For the first time, he realized that he actually hated exercise. Depressed and disappointed, he trudged after her, following but not seeing.

On Wednesday morning they arrived, as usual, Thomas, glum and despondent following her into the gymnasium lobby. He barely heard the sound of high pitched voices and the buzz of people. He changed into his gym clothes and followed her up the stairs to the weight room. The gym was busy, lines of people waiting for their turn to use the machines. It was overrun by local high school students. His wife abruptly turned around and almost walked over him.

"We're going home," she growled.

Thomas lurched sideways, and as he fell to the floor, he was sure he glimpsed his beauty talking to what has to have been her dark, slender sixteen-year-old boyfriend, also a beauty. "A couple from the garden of Eden!" he muttered to himself.

Someone was helping him up. It was the supervisor diligently trying to apply his knowledge of first aid to a victim who appeared to be in shock. Thomas felt his heart pulsate, pause too long, but then pick up again. He saw his beautiful image in 3D. The supervisor had lifted him onto his favourite weight machine, the one where he sat with his legs open. "Are you OK?" he heard.

"I'm perfectly fine," Thomas answered, a very faint, dreamy smile. He drank from a bottle of water and stood up of his own accord. She was waiting for him at the door.

As they exited through the gym lobby, she wanted him to stop at the desk and complain. The people at the Y were always helpful and courteous. Thomas hurried out, pretending not to hear her.

On Thursday Thomas went to the gym alone. She would not go until they did something about those students. He took the stairs to the weight room in leaps and bounds. But he knew already that it would not be as he wished. There was no noise of young lives. There were no students. He inquired at the desk. They came only on

Mondays, Wednesdays, and Fridays. He logged in and went through his monotonous routine. There were nine different machines to do. It was boring any time. Now it seemed an empty, useless chore. He sat down at his favourite machine and looked out at the vacant treadmill.

It was Friday morning, and Thomas was hurrying through his high fibre breakfast cereal.

"You're not going to the gym without me," she commanded, "and I'm not going to the gym until you do something about getting rid of those students."

She must suspect something, he thought, even though he hadn't done anything. But he had shaved much more carefully this morning and did get an expensive haircut yesterday. At his age of 69, he still had plenty of hair, most of it dark with just faint tinges of gray on the sides. Distinguished, he thought. And when he looked in the mirror this morning, he thought his diminutive features attractive and youthful – conveying a kind of energy that large lumbering people could not.

"OK," he said, "I think I'll go shopping instead."

On Monday, Thomas did something he had never done. With half a spoon of cereal in his mouth, he spluttered, "I'm going to the gym. It's bad for my health just sitting around."

She chewed on a piece of toast. He had tried to look her straight in the eye, but she was leafing through the latest specials in the supermarket lift-out of the Star and Banner daily. She didn't answer. He quietly picked up his gym bag and left. And soon he was bounding up the stairs three at a time and standing in line for his machine. Laughter filled the weight room. The students were back. And so was his couple. Eve sat back on the leg press, legs (such smooth tight skin) together pushing forward and releasing back as Adam stood by, looking down on her, counting her repeats.

"Slowly, slowly, you're going too fast," he said. Or was it Thomas who said that quietly to himself? Eve finished her set and Adam took her place. Thomas would be next. He gazed at Adam as in a trance. With rapture, he shifted his gaze to Eve who stood beside him. He drank in every piece of her gym clothes. The short tight pants reaching down her thighs, the old T-shirt with a worn out inscription and a small tear on the sleeve, and the cute sneakers striped with pink and matching laces. The boy was carefully groomed. Hair short and well-trimmed, a dark blue loose fitting track suit and stylish New Balance sneakers that supported a slender body and well-formed legs.

Nice! He reminded him of himself that once was! Thomas drove home that day twice failing to notice that the lights had turned green and was beeped by impatient motorists. But he didn't go straight home. Instead, he went shopping for a new set of gym clothes and sneakers.

Next morning at breakfast he announced to her that the students were still turning up at the gym and he had lodged a complaint with the gym manager. For fitness reasons, he had to go to the gym, but as a protest, he would go there only Mondays, Wednesdays, and Fridays until the matter was settled. In the meantime, he said to her, she should do something about maintaining her fitness too.

She glared at him. "I told you, I'm not going until the students are gone."

On Wednesday Thomas glided up the stairs but knew already that something was wrong. He heard only the steady drum of the treadmills. There were no students. He wandered around the weight room at a loss, not even following his strict sequence of machines. He sat down on his favourite machine, legs stretched out and apart, admiring his new sweat pants. They were tight like the ones cyclists wear. His legs and torso looked young! They were even attractive! At least he thought so. But he quickly rushed through his routines and casually asked the supervisor where the students were. He felt a sharp pain in his chest as he heard the answer. Their schedule had been changed. They came on the same days, but in the afternoons at 2.30 pm. His heart leaped, blood rushed to his face. He was short of breath.

Thursday was a memorable day because she kissed him! (Just a peck, mind you, much preferred by Thomas, because to be hugged by her could crush him). The kiss had been caused by the surprise Thomas had prepared for her. He had bought her a treadmill, and it had arrived that morning soon after breakfast. She would not have to go to the gym ever again. With great joy and excitement Thomas set it up for her, and she immediately took to it. And when she was done, he mentioned casually that he was going to change his time of going to the gym to the afternoons in order to avoid the students. He said it with apprehension and felt a tightness in his chest as he spoke. But she made no reply, which meant that it had worked. And the tightness in his chest faded.

Friday afternoon Thomas bounded up the gym stairs at exactly 2.30 pm. The noise level was back up, there was life in the weight room! Fewer people went to the gym in the afternoons, especially those who were seniors. They, of course, were home taking their naps. Not Thomas! There were no lines so he could go methodically through his regular routine, occasionally changing it if sitting on a particular machine would give him a better view of his beautiful couple. And they were a couple, he had no doubt. And as he worked out, he imagined them together.

On Monday afternoon Thomas sat at his machine. He had taken to doing extra sets, so occasionally there would be someone waiting to use it. He imagined that one time Adam or Eve would be waiting for him to finish. Perhaps he could stand up, wipe down the machine and just accidentally brush by one of them. He would feel his or her breath on his neck. His face flushed at the thought. And he felt the tightness in his chest, a dull ache in his arm, a faltering in his pulse. It was now 3.00 pm. and the students were there, but his couple was not. He slumped on the seat, drawing up his legs, knees pressed together.

"Excuse me," a voice came from somewhere above him. "Are you done? There are others who need to use that machine too, you know."

Thomas stood up too quickly and fell forward, striking his head on the floor. A bead of blood trickled from his nose.

"Are you OK? I didn't mean to scare you," Adam muttered as he leaned down to help Thomas up.

Thomas's eyes flickered and instantly brightened. He felt the firm grip of a well-conditioned arm under his.

"Of course I'm OK. I tripped over my new sneakers. I think they're a bit big for me."

He struggled to his feet and managed to graze his cheek against Adam's exposed upper arm. He smelled young, like a baby. The floor supervisor was on the spot, concerned about the blood trickling from Thomas's nose. "I'll call an ambulance," he said.

"Really, "there's no need. I'm fine. Just tripped over my own feet."

Thomas walked steadily to his next station. He looked for Eve and saw her coming across the room. Each step she took seemed as though in slow motion, like a fawn prancing through the air. A comfortable feeling of warmth seeped into his sweat pants, and, as his chest tightened, he was overcome by a messianic calm. Then he smelled the sweetness of her breath as his eyes closed, and a blind dropped from somewhere inside his head.

7. Seductio ad absurdum

A Roman love affair takes an unexpected turn

Julia always did have her head squarely on her shoulders, unlike Ella her elder sister by two years, who was flighty, unpredictable, highly strung, never stayed with one job or one boyfriend for longer than a month. Julia always seemed to know exactly what she wanted and where she was going. Her parents were therefore not at all surprised or distraught when Julia announced, at the tender age of twenty-two, the day after she graduated with her Bachelor of Arts, that she was going overseas and would back-pack across Europe. Two years ago, when Ella made a similar announcement, there had been a terrible scene, her mother imagining all kinds of disasters, especially of Ella falling into the hands of unscrupulous foreign lovers. These fears never surfaced when Julia made her announcement. No, mum and dad were delighted that Julia was going to "see the world" as countless young Aussies had been doing for decades. The fact was that almost all of them came back, settled down, got married and had kids. So Julia's mum and dad looked forward to a quiet couple of years, finding a modest place in Ocean Grove to which they could retire, and joining the local bowling club. They were both teachers, and both took the deal that many did in 1992, to retire at 50.

However, in Ella's case, her mom's fears were well founded, though she did not know it. Over the years Ella had been gone, Julia had received letters postmarked from many of the romantic spots of Europe, containing intimate details of her sister's lovers and their goings on. She read the letters over and over, kept them in a special drawer, and, especially when she was fed up with studying, loved lying on her bed, reading of Ella's more steamy episodes. She could never live her life like that, could not imagine how Ella could live her life moving from one aux pair job to another, or to put it bluntly, from one Baron's bed to another. This is not to say that Julia was narrow-minded, or overly moral about her sister's affairs. Not at all. How she longed to dabble in such fun! But a sensible girl knew that such activities must be kept in their place. The trouble was, she hadn't had any affairs to keep in their place. All she had were Ella's letters.

*

After her first year of gloom living in her bed sitter just around the corner from the British Museum, Julia managed to save enough money from her temporary typing job, to hitch-hike to Rome. There, she stayed with Ella who was currently out of work, having just finished a stretch as aux pair for an aristocratic family, or at least a family whose father was routinely addressed as "il Barone." That summer was an exciting period in which Ella introduced her to so many different people, and insisted on trotting her all over Rome and half of Italy visiting friends and seeing the sights. But there were no affairs. Maybe Ella, who was stunningly beautiful by the way, had made them all up in her letters. And yes, you guessed it, Julia was what people refer to as a plain looking girl, although there were times when one might catch sight of her from across the street, or looking down at her from the top of a flight of stairs, that her features were striking. The trouble was that when confronted with a man, especially one whom she might be attracted to, her face took on a fallen look; her nose seemed perhaps a little too straight and long; her chin too much a part of her neck, which was itself a bit too thick. This unfortunate plainness was not helped by her tendency to look down when talking to someone, a habit which she tried to avoid by not talking very much at all. It was why her father proudly described her as the strong, silent type.

All things considered, though, Julia's first European summer was a success. She managed to pluck one piece of experience out of that crazy three months, plucked it right out of the turmoil of a day she spent on the beach with a group of Ella's endless number of friends. While Julia squinted across the oily bodies, trying to appreciate the beauty of the medieval town of Sperlonga that jutted out over the sparkling water, her eye was attracted by a bronzed Italian body, scantily covered by a tiny white bikini. She found herself staring at him, unable to believe that he looked exactly like an Italian lover is supposed to look: dark, lightly silvered hair; a slightly pouting lower lip; black eyebrows and eyes; a slender body which moves powerfully and gracefully; feminine looking hands and feet. This gorgeous man was one of Ella's circle of friends. But was he not too beautiful for such a plain girl as Julia?

Considering this possibility, Julia lay back and closed her eyes. In her silent way, she resolved that she would have an affair with this man, no matter what. It would be her first. She may as well have herself deflowered by the most romantic man she could find!

Ella was accommodating and provided Julia with all the information she needed. Yes, she was lucky. Giulio was not married. Yes, he liked Anglo-Saxon girls. No, he was not a particularly pleasant person — vain, selfish, ill-tempered so there would be no chance of getting hooked on him. He also had two weekend houses, one by the beach, the other in the mountains. Was he good in bed? Ella drew the line there. Little sister would have to find that out for herself. And Ella, the same person who had written all those remarkable letters, gave her little sister a lecture on the risks involved in these affairs, especially for Anglo-Saxon girls in Rome.

"It's a trap," she said, shaking her finger at Julia. "Look at me. I'm stuck here, can't find any secure employment, I live from hand to mouth, yet I can't make myself leave this place."

What did that have to do with having an affair? Julia wanted to ask but didn't. She saw Ella's warnings as admissions on her part of having had so far no aim in life. As for herself, she planned simply a short, swift affair, without complications.

"Do you want to go out with him? I'm sure I could set it up for you, Julia."

"Oh no! Not so soon!" Julia replied, "but if you could arrange it so that we meet at a party or something, that will be enough."

Ella threw a goodbye party for Julia and invited Giulio. In front of a mirror, Julia practiced over and over the half dozen words she would say to him, forcing herself to stare directly into the eyes of her reflection. She would blush when she spoke to him, but told herself that this would probably tilt things in her favour, for he would no doubt infer from her shyness that she was a virgin. And this attraction would far outweigh her unattractive features.

On the night of the party, she was careful to wear a dress that could be seen as both provocative and conservative. She chose a long, white cotton dress, hand sewn from India, which, tied with a tan string tightly at the neck, draped down over her firm and well-proportioned breasts, was drawn in just enough to touch her hips, then hung loosely to the floor. The overall effect of this dress was to cover her completely, but also accentuate the better points of her body; enough for any man to want to see more.

The party was a great success, and everything went according to plan. Julia managed to stand alone for a period when she also saw that Giulio was alone. She stared self-consciously at the floor, her cheeks already flushed by the heat of the party. Suddenly he was in front of her, and, placing his feminine fingers under her chin, he gently lifted her head.

"Why are you so sad?" he asked in a romantic Italian-accented English.

"Oh! I'm sorry. I was just thinking." Julia forced herself to look into his dark brown eyes.

"You are looking forward to returning to London, no?" He smiled, and it was then that she noticed how perfectly manicured was his every feature.

"Yes. But I would very much like to return..." Julia's eyes flickered, but she forced them to stay where they were, "and perhaps we could see each other?"

"I would like that very much," he said, and immediately as he did so, Julia turned away, pretending that someone else had called her.

Now, she sat in the gloom of London's winter once again, waiting for her plan to work. She had sent him a postcard to his work address at the United Nations Information Office in Rome, marked merely with "Auguri," writing on it only her address and phone number.

Winter passed. Julia scrounged for money, lived on canned soup, toast, and eggs. Too shy to make friends, she read mountains of books to pass the time, being careful, of course, to choose those that would improve her intellect. She grew very lonely, and the only really "social" pass-time she had was writing letters home to her parents and the occasional letter to her sister. Gradually, she began not exactly to lie in these letters, but rather wrote them in such a way that they could be interpreted in the way her parents wanted: "...working in the famous Library of the British Museum..." Julia omitted to mention that it was a mind-deadening job of mending damaged books with sticky tape.

Now she came to understand a little better the letters that her sister had sent her. Spring arrived. And on the Wednesday before Good Friday, early in the morning she was awakened by the rough voice of the cleaning lady to say that she was wanted on the phone, long distance. It was Giulio.

"You must come for Easter," he said, not even waiting for Julia to say 'hello.'

"Er...yes, I'd like to, but I can't afford the airfare, I usually hitch-hike everywhere."

"Well, don't worry. Just borrow the money, and I'll pay for the flight." His voice purred with that lilting Italian accent. Julia was titillated.

"O.K. How will we meet?"

"Cable me your flight, and I'll pick you up at the airport."

"Fabulous. I'll see you soon."

"Yes, my carina, soon."

Julia did, in fact, have the money for the airfare. Expecting to be "sent for" at very short notice, she did everything she could to ensure that Giulio paid for his share of their pleasure. She bought a seat on an Easter charter flight, which cost half the price of the regular fare. Of course, she would not tell this to Giulio. And she had been on the pill for five months now, so that aspect of the affair was covered. Her case was already packed with expensive clothes; and she had bought him a present, a cute undershirt, white, with a black navel stamped on the front.

Nothing Giulio did surprised Julia. He met her at Ciampino airport and whisked her directly away to his beach house by Sperlonga. Their meeting seemed natural enough, and Julia, perhaps due to her keen anticipation of Giulio's wiles, was no longer shy. Indeed, she already felt as if she knew this man very well, observing his incredible vanity and his condescending manner, finding them amusing, and comforting; everything she had expected.

The hour ride to the beach house was uneventful. They spoke very little, and when they did, Julia asked most of the questions. Giulio was uncharacteristically quiet, and he played tape after tape of high-brow opera on his stereo cassette. Was Julia an opera enthusiast? Not exactly, she lied. Giulio was pleased.

Unfortunately, Julia's predictions began to go awry as soon as they arrived at Giulio's quiet beach house, which was hidden behind huge bushy oleanders, nestled into a small cove right on the beach front. Orange trees grew along the drive, a large palm stretched above the tile and stucco house. Giulio switched off the motor of the Alfetta, stepped out of the car and waited for Julia to alight. The first prediction wrong, he made no attempt to hold open the door for her. Instead, he threw her the house keys and said, "unload the car will you? I'm going for a run along the beach. There should be some spaghetti inside, and there are vegetables, and meat and everything else you'll need to make a sauce. See you in an hour or so." He pulled his sweater off over his head, blew her a kiss with his hand, then ran off through the sand.

Wrong again. Should he not have carried her inside and immediately thrust her into bed? But no! Italians first wine and dine their quarries by candle light and smooth talk designed to overcome the slightest misgivings of the purest fledglings. Julia, therefore, set about preparing a sumptuous meal of spaghetti with a green sauce that she had practiced especially for this occasion. She even found candles in one of the cupboards.

Julia waited for an hour and a half. If he didn't return soon, the candles would burn away. She put the spaghetti on, thinking that he would surely arrive any minute. Fifteen minutes went by, and she had to turn off the spaghetti. She blew out the candles and sat in the dark. All was silent except for the faint noise of the gently rippling sea. Another half hour went by, and Julia nodded off to sleep, sitting on a big cushion wedged into the corner of the small living room.

"Julia? Where are you? Where are you?"

Julia awoke with a start to hear Giulio's lilting voice.

"I'm here. I'm here," she replied as she groped for the light switch. She heard other voices too. A lot of them.

"Let's eat, Julia, we're all starving!"

Giulio pranced in, grabbed Julia in his arms and swung her around. Julia expected a kiss, but none came. She looked over his shoulder to see nine, maybe ten other people, all of whom she had probably met during her last summer's visit, but could not really remember.

"I've only cooked enough spaghetti for two," she whispered to Giulio.

"You've cooked the pasta already?" he asked mockingly. "How long did you cook the spaghetti?"

"Fifteen minutes, but..."

"Dio! Dio!" he laughed loudly, and the others laughed with him. "Never mind, I will cook the pasta. Julia, get the big pot from down there so we can boil the water."

Julia did as she was told.

"Now, amici, what sauce will we have?"

"I've prepared a green sauce, maybe we could add to it," put in Julia, red faced and embarrassed.

"Where? Let me smell it!" Giulio lifted the lid of the saucepan and immediately responded, "Humm! No pinoli...did you use fresh basilica?"

"No...I couldn't find any..."

"I have some in the garden. Amici, all out, to collect pinoli. We can't have green sauce without pine nuts."

Julia struggled to lift the enormous pot full of water onto the stove. Giulio strained the spaghetti she had cooked and said, "Mi dispiace, Julia, but this cannot be eaten by a civilized person. The rubbish bin is just out the back door. Would you please, my carina?"

Julia did as she was told.

Giulio's friends stayed all night, no one bothering to mention sleep until four in the morning. She had to admit, though, that his friends were extremely friendly, and treated her as if she had always been one of their group. There was not one hint of a snigger that she might be Giulio's latest conquest. Conquest indeed! Julia was at a loss as to how to behave next. She had expected to be swept off her feet. Yet, so far, Giulio had shown no physical closeness to her at all, merely paraded her around every now and again. She wondered whether he would ever take her to bed, wondering whether her anticipations were founded on utterly naive assumptions. Finally, completely exhausted, Julia found a comfortable rug in the corner of the living room and curled up to sleep.

A faint, soft voice purred, "Come, Julia my carissima, come! You'll be more comfortable in the bedroom."

Her body felt so heavy she was unable to get up. Then she felt Giulio's strong arms struggle with her dead weight, and someone else's, amidst muffled giggles, take up her legs. Soon she felt herself sinking deeper and deeper into the bed, feeling an enormous weight on top of her.

The weight stayed until she awoke amidst the noise of people getting breakfast. She looked across expecting to see Giulio beside her, but there was no one, nor did the bed seem as though he had slept there. In a mild panic, she put her hand on her crotch, realizing that she didn't know whether it had happened or not.

"Well! You're quite a sleeper. Would you like cappuccino or cafe?" Giulio's bright voice penetrated her preoccupation.

"Oh, Giulio! I, er, cappuccino, please. What time is it?"

"Ten-thirty! We are all going down for a swim. You come when you're ready. Ciao Carissima!"

"Ciao."

Their voices faded as they ran down to the beach. Julia felt around and discovered, with a sigh of relief, that she was intact. He hadn't touched her. She sat on the bidet and examined herself more carefully, unable to believe that he had left her alone. It was true. She looked in the bathroom mirror at herself and said, "Julia, this is ridiculous! You're relieved that he didn't and wish that he had! It's time to get out of this weird set-up." Thereupon, she attended to her toilet, made herself a cappuccino, and packed her case.

It was not until she had completed her packing that she realized there was no way to get back to Rome, except by thumbing a ride, as there were no buses over Easter. So she struggled with her bag up the steep alley that wound through the medieval fishing houses to the top of Sperlonga and booked into a hotel. There she sat for the rest of the day, too frightened to venture out. She began to write a letter to her parents, the gist of it being that she was spending Easter with a wealthy Italian couple who had a house in Rome, Sperlonga, and the mountains near Avezzano. "...he is an important United Nations official..."

Giulio and his friends arrived back at the house. They called for Julia, but Giulio saw that she had taken her bag and gone. He flew into a terrible rage, which his friends took to mean they were no longer wanted around. Then he cooked himself some pasta and took a nap. Julia sneaked out to buy a little pizza and saw Giulio's friends in a restaurant. She avoided them. At six o'clock there was a knock at her hotel room door, and Julia's heart leaped into her mouth. She opened it, and it was Giulio. He was smiling serenely, and she knew then that he wanted her to go back to the house.

"Carina! I'm very sorry. How could I have offended you? I have treated you with freedom, that is all! We must be free of each other, not like husband and wife. Capisci?"

Julia had not expected a speech. She had expected a command, and had readied herself to say "Yes." Instead, she gave him her bag.

"I am a woman," she said and stared as aggressively as she could into his dark eyes. The words and the stare seemed to bounce back at her, so she felt that she must continue. "The others ... are they still there?"

"No, I asked them to leave. They understand, my carina. Now let us go."

Giulio led the way down the stony alley, Julia following him, somewhat sullenly. She had not felt this weird mixture of resentment and compliance since she was a child being ordered to do something by her mother. Giulio walked faster and faster so that Julia had to trot and stumble to keep up. She wanted to smack him.

They entered the house. Giulio locked the door and closed the shutters. He threw her bag across the room and turned to her, his upper lip slightly curled.

"My carissima. You wish to be treated as a woman?"

"I ...I... don't think I meant it that ... way," Julia stammered.

"Come to me."

Julia did as she was told. Giulio took her in his arms and kissed her so hard it hurt her lips, then ran his mouth down to the side of her neck and bit her so hard it drew blood.

"Oh!" she cried. "Stop it!"

Giulio did not stop. He stepped back and gave her a sharp crack across the face with his open hand, sending Julia staggering towards the bedroom door. She crouched down, cowering. Giulio this time kicked her in the chest.

"You English women are all the same. You think you are so fine you want it to be torn from you, you can't think of doing it any other way."

Julia crawled away, cringing at another blow he landed on her buttocks. She scurried under the bed, trying to work out what to do.

"Come out whore! Come out, and I'll get done what you came here for!" Julia would not come out. This was not her idea of an affair, not at all. She lay there curled up, small tears forming in her eyes, slowly trickling down her cheeks. Giulio yelled and banged the bed; dropped down to his knees to show her his weapon, but she closed her eyes tightly. He promised to the point of pleading that he would not hurt her; tried moving the bed, but she moved right along with it. Julia waited, and even toyed with the idea of coming out to face him. She was after all bigger than he, and might even be able to overpower him. But no. Julia lay there a long time until finally, she heard the engine of Giulio's Alfetta roar to life, and stones hit the side of the building as the wheels spun in the gravel. He was gone.

Feeling suddenly light-hearted, she struggled out from under the bed, quite sure in herself that Giulio would not return. It was dark again, so she lit the candles and treated herself to a plate of spaghetti al Ragu, then curled up on the sofa with a stimulating book on the history of art. Tomorrow she would lie on the beach in the warm Mediterranean sun and finish her letter home.

8. Head's Up

Sex obsessed Jones turns on himself

DECAY: Indicates deteriorating change, often gradual, from a sound condition or perfect state.

Jones shook his head as he copied the definition into his dog-eared notebook. Not only was this definition too vague, but it was also clearly wrong. Who is to say that a live body is in a perfect state? Doesn't the decomposition into the simplest elements suggest a return to a perfect state? As people get older, don't they get smarter and wiser?

The librarian was coming. He closed the book, and placed *Sex as Bait* on top of it, as he always did. He had found *Sex as Bait* by chance as he vainly browsed the shelves looking for books that might have some hot content. Unlikely in a local public library, of course. But one never knows. Every now and then a title might slip through the bespectacled lens of the library acquisitions committee. It was a book full of psychobabble, a great disappointment. But the cover title, a plain yellow cover with *Sex as Bait* printed in bold black letters was all he needed. Her denim trousers brushed against the corner of his table as she cruised quietly by. He wiped his sweaty hands on his pants, letting his body slide further under the table. She suspected him, he was sure of it. He had borrowed then returned *Sex as Bait* every week for the past three months. She pretended not to notice.

The lights dimmed. Five minutes before closing. And just getting dark outside too. This was it. Now or never! Jones moved to stack away his books and notes, rummaged around in his raincoat, which was draped over the back of his chair. He slipped it on, the revolver weighing the pocket down, so. he stepped into the bathroom, stuck the gun in his belt, then changed his mind and put it back in his coat pocket. He tried not to look in the mirror. His wife and three kids, what about them? "All in all, they'll be better off for it," he mused. Anyway, he no longer had a choice in the matter. He was driven by a force within, as though someone else had taken over his body., a kind of out-of-in-body experience. He rearranged his pants again, buttoned just one button of his raincoat, then emerged from the bathroom. Everyone had left except the librarian who stood with her tight buttocks facing him. Jones sighed nervously, pulling his coat together at the front. She turned and smiled.

"Good night, Mr. Jones."

Jones nodded imperceptibly and trotted out the door.

He waited in the bushes to the side. The sky darkened, and a light drizzle descended. Jones looked with satisfaction at his raincoat. His body bled inwardly, heat steamed from his cheeks. The sweat oozed out of his arm pits and tickled as it made its way down. His crotch was on fire. There was little time. And what there was of it could not be stopped.

The drizzle stopped, and a faint spring breeze rustled the azaleas. Jones gritted his teeth as the lights in the library went on again. "She must have forgotten something," Jones muttered to himself. God, Mrs. Jones, if you only knew! But how could you? I know you don't have time either. You're at the school track meet, at piano lessons, gymnastics, or baseball practice, and there's a PTA meeting tonight. Don't forget that, and the kids have to do their homework, and no I haven't got time to fix your bike, because there's the broken window out the back, and there's the shopping, and the lawn to mow, the car, the bills, and the school board meeting, and I promised to drive the Cub Scouts to the park.

The lights were going out again. Soon she would appear on the steps, stretched denim buttocks, slender arms bare only to the elbows. She won't understand why I'm going to do this. No one would, so there's no sense my trying to explain. Oh! But the day your fingers just grazed my knuckle when I handed you my library card! If only you could know how I have suffered ever since! A tragic path from meagre beginnings!

He saw his kids playing kickball in the street. Heard them complain when told it was time for bed. Mommy would read them a story. Eat up your supper! Sit up straight! Goddamn you, don't bang the plates!

The heavy metal door of the old library clanged shut, and the librarian stood briefly at the top of the bluestone steps, enjoying the scent of the azaleas. She would hang on to the left rail as she always did, taking one step at a time, the stretched denim giving way to flesh and muscle.

She would pass the largest of the azalea bushes behind which stood Jones, red and bursting.

Now she was so close, he could put out his hand and grab her. "God Almighty! Here I come!" he screamed to himself, sniffing like a dog for her scent. It's bed time, kids...the story's over, this is the last time. He thrust his hand into his loose coat pocket, grasping the gun. The other hand had already unzipped his pants. She came by, and he jumped out intending to make a resounding battle cry. He stood in front of her, his pants around his ankles, coat wide open; an enormous erect confrontation, better than he had dreamed.

Pandemonium.

She screamed and ran blindly onto the road. People came running, cars screeched to a halt. A police siren sounded in the distance. He shook the revolver loose from his pocket and, looking down, took careful aim. He had practiced this many times behind the locked door of his bathroom.

Bang! The head was gone and with it the body.

9. Parodisiac

A student mocks his professor with love and envy

Unashamedly, I write of the affinity between flowers and students. The buds slowly open, the petals unfurl voluptuously. They are ripe for action. Pearls of wisdom fall like droplets on the beckoning flower. This exotic moment in time is an eternity for students who believe they are lush growing plants, but to the teacher they are but cut flowers, objects of passing beauty, replaceable.

"They will droop and die a rotten, smelly death," Vanillino, my dear professor would say later, the smell of beauty overpowering the stifling smoke of cigarettes in our tiny classroom. It was the 1960s, and the world was on fire, especially in America. But I learned from Vanillino that a journey was a religious venture, a pilgrimage, which was the last thing I had imagined when I set out for America from half way around the world. A journeyman lives like a cultural parasite wherever he stops. He sails through the turbulence, aware but unaffected. Unless, of course, he meets someone like Vanillino.

In class, I took notes with difficulty. "I can't think of anyone who does not yearn for acceptance," he says, speaking of his idol, Jean Genet. "My being a judge is the emanation of being a thief.." He pauses, a trickle of saliva creeps from the edge of his mouth, "…even He, who rejected our world, wanted acceptance…" My notes are smudged, I think there is something scrawled about an "outsider" To be frank, I remember little of what he said. I was just enthralled with his overbearing presence. Such a big man, standing tall with his shoulders held back, the sexy stiffness of a soldier maybe, loping sideways, occasionally swiveling to the blackboard where he scrawled words—useless words—that he must have expected me to write down. A drooping flower asked a question. It was something about existentialism, another stupid word. Vanillino responded gripping his white handkerchief which, squashed into a tiny ball, he continually passed from hand to hand. His pungent, sweaty palms were ripe for action. Oh, the luscious beauty of it all! I pushed my own hands forward on the table in front of me. I imagined him with one arm, placing his wet hand flat on the table. Then I would slowly move mine to his, gently turn his hand over to reveal what I knew was there—the stigmata of a saint!

The blackboard was full of tables and diagrams. Vanillino had written a book—the first of many. There were circles, arrows, and squares containing much text. I searched for meaning but could find only the delicious smudges from the ooze of his hands. I was jealous. Vanillino was in love with his words and could care less about us. I recoiled at his callousness, but then I had learned from Him that I should rejoice in it. "Find the beauty of His world which is the real world," Vanillino had told us. I searched unsuccessfully for the beauty in Vanillino's world, I really tried. But his words strangled and suffocated me as in a climax. Sex accentuated every syllable. His pink lips reveled in them, his tongue supplying them with ample spit, which he occasionally but unintentionally shared with us. We sat silent, our hands under the table. We were ripe too. But Vanillino was far away. He was in his world and we in ours. And the more distant, the more he attracted our adoration. And the more worship I gave, the more resistant I became. We began to argue. We were like lovers.

He was a bully. Yet he never laid a hand on me, something that I regret to this day. Indeed, he seems never to have laid a hand on anyone, even in war, a fact that I could not comprehend. A man so big, so big he could fill a room as soon as he entered it, especially a room full of others. When I sat in his classroom, I was cowed into insignificance. "I was crushed by his mass of flesh." I made myself love it and looked forward to each class where I could lose myself in his overpowering verbosity and sweat while at the same time despising his total disregard for my love. I later punished him mercilessly for this when I joined with my own students to gang up on him in his tiny Boston apartment just around the corner from Harvard. For Vanillino had run there to worship at the feet of the great anointed. He had sat at the feet of B.F. Skinner (or so he said). I had discovered that, outside the classroom, grovelling was his primary strength. He had learned how to do it when he was a prisoner of war, cooking gourmet meals for his captor. Oh, how I engineered so many situations in which he cooked for me! And he did. I took great pleasure in every bite, but even more pleasure at leaving him late at night with the piles of oily pots and pans and my plate that I had purposely left filthy, a used Kleenex dropped carefully on a gnawed skeleton of a fish. My student, Robert, whom Vanillino thought he had stolen from me, mercilessly attacked him, dissecting his every word. These Boston meetings became screaming matches, the pitch of Vanillino's voice rising to a shriek, accusing us of ignorance, we accusing him of playing God. When we left his presence, we sniggered to each other. It seemed that the more we attacked him, especially my tall and slender Robert, often leaning into Vanillino, and the more he did it, the more Vanillino loved him for it. The next day he would cook us a wonderful dinner, and we would leave the dirty dishes for him to lovingly clean. This was surely a Heaven of cut flowers. It could not last, and did not. My faithful Robert, collaborator in torture, suffered a violent death and everything collapsed as it was supposed to. Vanillino and I lost touch with each other. We could not speak of such cruelty.

*

We met again in Paris. I was arrested at the airport. They had heard of my dirty past no doubt. We saw each other through the glass that separated the insiders from the outsiders. He relished my exclusion, and it was not until I was about to enter the plane to be deported back to America that he stepped in to save me. He had whined all day when we spoke on the phone. Why had I not obtained a visa? Did I not want to see him? He mocked me through the glass, head held back, that straight, stiff soldier's body, a pose he used to make him seem even larger than he was. Vanillino had always "known" people in high places in many governments. One of these was the Paris, police commissioner. After he had enjoyed my suffering, stuck between in and out, he exerted his influence, and I was "in" so quickly, retrieved like a piece of lost baggage.

We had to meet in Paris. All that existentialism he had preached had made it inevitable. He ran around the streets and alleys of the Sorbonne (always the Sorbonne where I dutifully listened to him tell of famous French intellectuals who ate here, pissed there, fucked somewhere). He had gathered around him a motley crew. He had seduced many. A mathematician for his numbers, which he used in his papers to make them scientific; an actress, a playwright, whatever. We ran from one café to another, one bookshop to another and it seemed that, like a dog, he pissed on every corner, telling all Paris that he was there, right there in his rightful place. So appropriate that it was his dick that led us through the streets of Paris. Except that his dick had other things on its mind. Abruptly, Vanillino left me stranded. He went back to Israel for prostate surgery. Why there? Why not have it knifed right there where I would have held his hand or even the knife? Those charming days in Paris. After he had gone, I went back and followed the scent he had left. I sat in the cafés; speculated on being and nothingness, but all I could think of was *Sex as Bait*. This was Paris after all. The bait hung in the air on every sidewalk café, and it reeked of suspicion, for I knew that Robert had spent himself here with Vanillino. I had no evidence, but suspicion was enough. It just wasn't the same without Robert who was gone. But what would become of Paris without Vanillino? Was it the end of Vanillino?

*

He beckoned me once again. I followed him to an island that I imagined could be held in one of Vanillino's puffy hands. It was an island swelled by its own importance. And Vanillino had become the confidant of the University's Rector to whom he had made many promises; none of which could possibly be kept. They clearly were "into" each other; Vanillino the liar and bully, and the Rector, a cunning, well-scrubbed priest, fascinated by Vanillino's love of words, which the Rector twisted and turned to his advantage. Vanillino used words because he lusted for them. The Rector used words to penetrate others. Theirs was a matrimonial coupling. Vanillino made more promises to the Rector who seemed to believe them. We retired to an outdoor café, and I ate pastizzi. Vanillino was resplendent in his new denim jacket that he had bought at the market for $5 after a lot of haggling. He showed it off, thinking it made him look Bohemian and youthful. But he did not look a bit like Vanillino. And I was jealous of the Rector.

"It's too small for you," I said. He was shocked.

"Then I'll take it back and change it."

"You can't do that after so much haggling. Besides, it looks perfect. I was just joking."

Oh, the joy of Vanillino squirming! How foolish he looked with the jacket buttoned so tightly, his aging abdomen pushed down, enlarging his hips as those of a woman! I took a large bite of my pastizzi and chewed it sloppily with my mouth open. He sipped his tea. He could not eat pastry because of his diabetes, which delighted me no end. He took a deep breath and his soldier's shoulders squared up, his chest straining the studs of his new jacket. He was angry, and I was hot for it. This would not be the end of it. He would remember this as he remembers everything he has ever done or thought, everything that others have done to him. Every little detail he remembers. So he would get back at me for this. For how can one forgive if one cannot forget? Vanillino does not forgive. He accumulates slights, like the underground man. It is his bloated memory that makes him such a big man.

Malta was full of pale English women, too old to be single, but they were. Two came into the hotel restaurant as we sat having our breakfast. We were discussing the Stockholm prize. Vanillino was wearing his new jacket. He stood immediately they entered, welcoming them, praising their beauty, especially their hair. He liked hair. After pleasantries, he began the real charm. I sat still, sulking, and annoyed at this interruption, even though I had known for many years that this was Vanillino after all. It was a life of constant interruptions; every routine activity was a stage for Vanillino. Women, no matter how ugly, were his props. They sat at the table across from us. (My teeth are clenched as I write this, it annoys me so.) He sized them up exactly. Young women, eager for excitement, unlucky in love. Nearly too old for it. Vanillino offered an exciting moment, and I sensed even as I sat sullenly picking at my eggs and bacon in silence, that one of them (the larger, fulsome one with the knitted sweater) would go to bed with him at that very moment. Had he been doing this to make me jealous, I would have loved him for it. But he was doing it because he was Vanillino and was incapable of doing otherwise. Vanillino, the existentialist, was hooked on others, he was ripe for them, always in season.

We argued all day at the meeting in which we were to design a research project on some hot subject and bring in millions of dollars to the university. Vanillino left the next morning ostensibly to attend to a family crisis. I was left with the hotel bill to pay. The Rector had paid nothing for the meeting or the trip. It had cost him nothing. He would get nothing in return. And I was left licking my wounds, lovingly inflicted by Vanillino.

*

Body searches happen in Israel at Tel Aviv airport, so I am told. I thought of Vanillino being stripped and searched. He would request a female stripper, no doubt. I had followed him yet again, this time to Jerusalem. We were put up at Kibbutz Male Hamisha just outside of Jerusalem, atop a steep hill of many, surrounded by small Arab villages built around restaurants that catered to tourists. But Vanillino could hardly be seen, and when he was, he was unrecognizable, resplendent in a dark navy suit, spotless white shirt with stiff collar, and a striped blue tie. The suit did for him what convict garb did for Genet, exposing his duplicity, his profound potential for violence. It frightened me, and I kept away. I saw him only once return to who he was, when in the middle of a crowded restaurant that boasted authentic Israeli cuisine (weeds gathered from the hills of Jerusalem), he stood tall, tie removed, back arched, fondling the hair of one of his many female admirers who were lined up awaiting his caresses and his predictable compliments on their irresistible femininity. They struggled against each other to reach him, and I was overjoyed to suffer the stains of their excitement when one of his more ugly admirers knocked over a bottle of red wine, splashing my pants wherein lay the source of my envy. Turmoil erupted, and suddenly Vanillino fell to abusing one of the Latinos in our party who was complaining about the food. I timidly withdrew from the din and abuse which was Israel. I had no place there. And Vanillino had no time for me. Anyway, in his suit, he wasn't Vanillino.

The truth is that a chasm had opened between us. I had made what I thought was a humorous speech of adoration in front of all his anointed luminaries. I called him God which must have been a blasphemy because one of his suited admirers convinced him that I had done him wrong. What greater expression of worship and recognition could I have given him but to call him Augustus? Perhaps dropping to my knees before him would have made the difference. But how does one make a speech kneeling down? I could have washed his feet, I suppose. But then the audience may have misinterpreted my actions just as it apparently had my words. I never said goodbye, and I left with a sense of foreboding.

*

Two weeks after nine-eleven I followed Vanillino yet again, this time to Trier, where much of ancient Rome's money was minted and where the Crusaders massacred Jews because they could not find any Arabs. Here Vanillino could be Caesar. Money, after all, was the flavour of his tongue. Through it (or his claimed lack of it) he refined his snivelling, grovelling, whining self-respect. This was his envy, and he could not get enough of it just as he could not get enough adoration. In fact, it is hard to tell the difference between him and money, they define each other so deeply. I say these things of him because I love him, they are his endearing qualities. I would have him no other way. These are not character flaws or faults, they are his authentic human traits to be loved and caressed by his real friends. They attest to his honesty and to mine. We were lost in Trier, our German hosts most kind and forthcoming with a bounty of wine. Vanillino informed them that nine-eleven was the result of the clash of civilizations. It was Israel made big throughout the world. Our German hosts were still smarting from the clash of civilizations that was World War II. It was at this time that Vanillino became a Jew. Clearly, this was in order to put the Germans on the defensive so he could win his argument. Vanillino would stop at nothing to gain preeminence. Terrorism was in the air, though. Vanillino was used to it, and he knew the enemy.

*

When the Hamas guy leaped out of his seat, I shrank down into mine. Vanillino and I were together in Istanbul, lovers once again. Would his big frame protect me, stop a bullet? The panel of religious leaders harangued and argued among themselves, oblivious to Hamas. Vanillino did nothing. I nudged him (one of the few times I touched him) and said, "You have to stop this guy. He'll kill someone." "I know, I know," he said. It was his opportunity to show me how big he really was. But he did nothing. There was a faint rumble as people squirmed in their seats and scraped the floor with their feet. Mr. Hamas, occupying a seat, dead centre of the auditorium, pushed his way to the aisle, still yelling. I noted calmly his nicely pressed pants, and sports jacket carefully ironed white shirt with an open neck. He left, still yelling. The religious leaders prattled on. Vanillino said, "Let's go to the Grand Bazaar."

I had thought of buying a carpet. Vanillino had insisted that the Grand Bazaar in Istanbul was the place to do it. He would handle all the haggling for me. He was an expert and would save me hundreds of dollars. I believed him. Haggling was part of his personality, his persistent whining like a dog gnawing a bone that had been long stripped of meat. The haggling began with the taxi, which should have been a warning to me. There were five of us so the driver would not take us all in the taxi, "against the law," he says. So Vanillino pays him double to squeeze us in. I trot along behind Vanillino through the labyrinth, hawkers, chasing, following us, others standing at the entrance to their shops, purring with enticing promises.

"This is a good friend of mine," Vanillino says, and ushers us into a narrow doorway, festooned with carpets and rugs of many sizes and colours. We are all seated and offered tea. This I know Vanillino loves. After me, tea is his greatest pleasure. The sales pitch begins. Rugs are unfurled with flare. We are taught the finer points of carpet making and how to tell good from bad carpets. Very entertaining. Vanillino is in his element. The salesman asks which one I want. "The prices are very high," I say. Vanillino ignores me. "How grand the carpets are," he mumbles to himself. No haggling. I remain mute. The salesman drops his price. I say nothing. Vanillino is supposed to bargain. He does not. We are shown more, cheaper rugs. I begin to get annoyed and stand as if to leave. I'm sweating under the hot lights, even more than Vanillino. We are offered more tea which Vanillino eagerly accepts. I decline. Just as the tea arrives, I get up to go. Vanillino is aghast.

"I've decided I don't want a carpet," I say.

"But they've given us tea," he says, "you have to buy one, and the prices are good."

I look at him, incredulous. "You were supposed to haggle."

"I didn't have to!"

"Whose side are you on?"

I look around the room, the rest of our colleagues sit sniggering.

"Alright! Alright!" he cries.

I am already gone, trying to get out as quickly as possible. Then I'm lost in the alleys of the bazaar. Turning one way, then the other. I buy a teapot. Suddenly I find myself at one of the many exits. Not like Sartre, I grin to myself. Vanillino will not leave me. I feel him standing behind me, and I turn. I have lost him once again.

*

The grandeur of crumbling marble edifices, columns barely upright, bits of stone lying where they had fallen many years ago, invokes a sad yearning for the past, an authentic story of love. And here we were again, Vanillino and I, seated at the table of one of the Sicilian Mafia. There were just four of us and our host seated at a long table in a grand hall, surrounded by musty old drapes, the walls seeming to bend under their weight. Waiters stood back, adorned in their white powdered wigs (actually no longer powdered, now the colour of light tea), their dull satin uniforms showing their age. Our host spoke no English, I a little Italian (useless in this part of Sicily anyway), and of course, Vanillino showed off his perfect French. Our host, Salvezza da Drenaggio waived his arm and coughed up a few sentences, to which his personal assistant who sat by his side, so close he was almost sitting on his lap, laughed loudly, shouting, "That's right boss, that's right!" He looked straight at us, We had to laugh too, nodding our heads as we chomped away on Sicilian roast lamb. I could not detect exactly what was said, but I thought I heard something about blood on the steps. How could that be funny without being dreadful?

Salvezza's ragazzo accompanied us in what seemed to be an official car, equipped with a flag and diplomatic plates of some kind, to our hotel in Siracusa. It was late at night as we passed through small villages perched on steep hillsides, our car flanked on four sides by motor cycle police, their sirens blaring. The car stopped, not at our hotel, but at the mountain of steps leading up to the Town Hall. We were to be shown something. "Here! Look this!" the ragazzo shouts in English, smiling broadly. He shines his flashlight on the Town Hall steps, and there we see clearly the dark brown stains of blood that had run down several steps.

Vanillino stiffened. "Alright! Alright!"

"What's the matter?" I say.

"It's where the previous mayor was gunned down." Vanillino says proudly. "A bullet in each arm and leg, his prick and balls cut off and stuffed in his mouth. Then a knife to the heart. These guys don't fool around."

"Which guys?" But Vanillino is already in the car, calling to our laughing ragazzo in French to take us to our hotel.

We said our good nights and went up to our rooms. But I saw him leave directly after. He had a meeting with someone else whom I knew he had phoned earlier in the day. This was Vanillino, the lush, full blown flower, petals browning with age but clinging to the stem, still anchored, past cutting.

*

I have reached the point where there is little more to say, or at least nothing new to convey. for now, I see that every event has a monotonous similarity with every other. In fact, reading back through these words that I have vomited and sometimes spat onto these pages, I am sorely tempted to erase everything and replace it with a photograph of the two of us, carefully arranged as in a vase of flowers. That I did not is further confirmation of my cowardly love in the face of Vanillino.

10. A Meeting of Relatives

A famous anthropologist unravels the primitive mind

Dr. Lewis Berger was an anthropologist who became famous in the 1950s for his daring expeditions into the depths of dark continents and other far-away places. He was the first, and sometimes only, white man that many of the lost tribes of his discovery ever knew. Dr. Berger's fame also arose from his great humanism. He was always concerned that, by bringing these Primitive Peoples into contact with Western Civilization, their cultures would be destroyed, their "souls ripped from their bodies." Therefore, when he judged that a particular tribe was, on balance, living as happily or more happily than the people of his own culture (Oxford, England), he thereby left them alone and refused to give up any information as to where they might be found. Naturally, this led to lots of criticism from his fellow anthropologists, because it required him to conduct many of his expeditions in deep secrecy. There was no way of establishing the "validity of his findings," as they say in social science. Matters were made even more difficult for Dr. Berger when it came to convincing funding agencies to finance his expeditions since they were simply not courageous enough to risk their money on "some wild safari," as one evaluator so coarsely put it. And Dr. Berger wrote so colourfully, many suspected that he sat underneath one of those shady date palms, the exciting sounds of the jungle around him, and dreamed it all up. None of these things concerned Dr. Berger one scrap. In fact, they played into his hands since all he wanted was to "lead" lone expeditions, which cost, comparatively speaking, very little money—just sweat and exertion on his part.

Dr. Berger's last expedition was into the jungles of central Indonesia, where he had heard of a fierce tribe of head hunters that had resisted, indeed repelled, all attempts by explorers and even the soldiers of the Indonesian government, to penetrate the seclusion of their villages. There is little doubt that Doctor Berger, somehow, slipped into this tribe and lived among them for some time.

The full story of his disappearance will never be known because it was three years before anyone became alarmed that something may have happened to him: people had become used to his many secret and solitary withdrawals from civilization. In reconstructing the events that led to the doctor's disappearance, I have had to rely on the rare jabberings of his friend, Ockabunga, who was one of the tribe's young leaders. Snippets of the Doctor's field notes were found sewn into Ockabunga's delicately feathered head-dress, and these have been of inestimable value. For the rest, I have had to imagine it:

Friday, June 14, 1959
After five days tracking around the colourful ghettoes of Djakarta, I at last found a capable native of the Ung Fungo tribe who agreed to be my guide for six pence a day, meals provided. This tribe is thought to have contact with the Folijot warriors. The sun is baking me, the sky seems white hot. But this is the dry season, so at least I'm thankful that the steam of the tropics isn't yet closing in.

Thursday, July 30, 1959
A quick note. Have walked for days and days, chopping our way through grass, 8 to 10 feet high. Snakes, reptiles, all those animals that slink about. The stench from black mud under foot. It's like Hell, the sun's heat penetrates even the thickest cover. My guide Tojo doesn't even sweat. Sings a monotonous tune over and over. I'm getting old. May turn back. Exhausted—

*

No field notes describe Doctor Berger's first encounter with the Folijot warriors, although we are relatively sure that his guide abandoned him in fear, and that he remained alone in the jungle for several days, resting and gathering his strength. In what follows, I have reconstructed what I think may have occurred.

When he was searching for a snake that he could kill for food, Dr. Berger pushed back a large succulent leaf, and there standing before him was Ockabunga, short and stocky, with fatty breasts, a huge smile on his face; a forehead that reminded Doctor Berger of the pictures he had seen of prehistoric man.

"How do you do, I'm Doctor Lewis Berger."

"!" replied Ockabunga, laying his spear aside, and extending the other hand out in a friendly gesture.

Ockabunga was a man of few words, his most common one being a deep grunting sound that came from somewhere in his chest. No english phonics reproduce the sound accurately, so I will use the notation "!" when it is necessary to represent it.

From Doctor Berger's notes, and from what we now know about the Folijot warriors, it remains a mystery as to why the natives received Doctor Berger when they had so violently rejected all others. And Doctor Berger a white man, too! My own theory is that Ockabunga fell in love with Doctor Berger, in the sense that he was fascinated by the Doctor's toothless smile, reddish sunburnt skin, and twinkling eyes. It seems that Doctor Berger moved in with Ockabunga and that they developed, what one might call, an intimate relationship:

*

Tuesday, October 22, 1959

I have been unable to communicate with Ockabunga except on a physical level. He has said, perhaps, no more than 3 different words to me. Physically, however, he is most forthright. Each night after a large meal of juicy meat and vegetables, we sit in front of his grass hut, sipping coconut juice. I talk and talk and talk, telling him of the wonders of our civilization. He nods his head, smiles, grunts. Then, after some hours, he leans toward me, grips my arm firmly and grins widely. We go into his hut and lay on his straw mat together—

December 1959

We talked about medicine last night. Ockabunga seems very interested. I drew diagrams for him, he got excited, pulled me into bed. The Folijot sex and kinship patterns are still a complete mystery. I have so far seen no women or children. This small village of 12 huts, arranged in a circle, houses 24 young men of Ockabunga's age. One of them goes off into the jungle and returns with cooked food each day. I have asked to see the women and children, but Ockabunga pretends he doesn't understand me. Yet I know he does. His eyes are frightening, they are so lucid and penetrating. During our evening talks, he sometimes looks at me as if he knew it all and much more. Very unnerving—

March 1960

— I'm losing track of time. Dates no longer matter. The lethargy induced by tropical heat, and my liaison with Ockabunga, is destroying my soul. He's no longer an exotic native. I hate him. He's kept me, prisoner, all this time, and I've only now understood this. I have resolved that tomorrow, I won't go to bed with him.

*

The remainder of Doctor Berger's notes is scribbled furiously, often both horizontally and vertically across the same page. Most of it is illegible, none of it is dated. I have tried to piece together the remains of his field notes along with my own interviews with Ockabunga to construct the rest of the story.

It seems that the next evening, when Ockabunga beckoned Doctor Berger into his hut, the doctor said, "No!" Ockabunga replied, "!!" and sat down again. He pointed to the doctor's mouth, to his throat, to his own head, then traced a shape on the ground. The doctor quickly recognized that Ockabunga was, at last, communicating positively, he wanted to be educated. The doctor was elated, immediately began to teach Ockabunga to speak English, and in only a few months, Ockabunga was speaking it, "like a native," as they say.

Then it was Doctor Berger's turn to be educated. He was taken head hunting, taught how to stalk another native, how to chop off the head leaving enough skin on the neck, so that when the head was boiled in special herbs, the skin had room to shrink, and settled smoothly over the hardened flesh of the cheeks.

"When will I see the women and children?" Berger asked.

"When you have cut off your first head," replied Ockabunga.

Many months went by. The good doctor could not, of course, bring himself to kill someone and cut off his head. He wanted to leave this tribe and get back to civilization. The more he learned about their language and lifestyle, the more he began to hate them, Ockabunga especially. This upset him because he had never felt this way about the many tribes he had previously discovered. He had always felt a special kind of love for them. He never judged them, he always accepted them for what they were. His role was not that of judge, but of scientist and humanist.

One day, Ockabunga touched his arm gently—the first time he had touched him since the doctor's loud rejection—and smiled:

"Today you will see your first child," he said. "And as well you may have your own hut and may take in your own companion. We will have a feast to celebrate."

The doctor was both pleased and worried. He had waited so long to see this child. But he was being moved out from under Ocka- bunga's protective wing.

The feast began. Two natives emerged from the jungle carrying a large wooden dish, garnished with big banana leaves, and in the middle, the still sizzling, dark brown child, the legs trussed up under the chin, roast yams spaced around the dish, a paw-paw slice wedged into the mouth. Cheers of approval went up from the tribe.

The doctor feigned illness, which was not so difficult under the circumstances. He emerged from his hut several days later, weak and emaciated from lack of food. Ockabunga approached him.

"Come back to my hut," he said. "I don't think you are ready yet."

And the Doctor gathered up his things and moved back in with his host. The days passed, the doctor regained his strength, and with it, his resourcefulness. He had realized that many bodies were going to waste. He looked around Ockabunga's hut and counted 63 heads of all shapes and sizes, as well as 37 skulls. The bodies could be made use of. He would teach Ockabunga some anatomy.

That evening, they sat in front of Ockabunga's hut, as they had done now every night for over two years. It was hot, steamy, and the insects buzzed around the little camp fire. The soft smell of the straw mats on which they sat oozed upward, mixing with the odour of their bodies. Ockabunga had one of those all-knowing looks in his eyes.

"!" he said.

"Have you ever taken the time to look inside these corpses that you throw away?" asked Doctor Berger.

"We want only the heads. They have the spirit."

"That may be true." Doctor Berger paused, realizing that perhaps he should begin his anatomy lesson with the part of the body in which the Folijot were most interested. "Now take the human brain," he continued, pointing to his own head, "it's the most amazing part of our bodies. "Yes, it is the spirit," nodded Ockabunga, looking wise.

"It's more than that, Ockabunga. Do you know that it's made up of millions of tiny little cells that turn on and off, and talk to each other in electricity? You remember what I told you about electricity, don't you?"

"Yes."

"The brain controls all the rest of the body, you know. It receives electrical impulses, processes them, then sends messages back. You see? When I raise my hand, my brain has told it to do so." The doctor tapped his head with his finger to emphasize the point.

"Different parts of the brain control different parts of the body. The front part here, for example, controls speech, and the amazing thing is that the right side controls the left side of the body, and the left the right, isn't that amazing?"

Then Doctor Berger broke his rule never to make an advance to a native. He reached across and stroked Ockabunga's cheek with his open palm. "Tomorrow, or the next time when you bring in a head, we must cut it up, and I'll teach you what is inside. What do you think of that?"

"!" said Ockabunga, and he rose up, stretched his hand down and softly felt all over the Doctor's head. Then he walked over to his long spear which was leaning against the hut. Their eyes met, and the Doctor was frightened by the all-seeing clarity of Ockabunga's gaze. There was no silly grin. "No simple savage this," thought Doctor Berger, as Ockabunga raised the spear carefully, then thrust it deep into the Doctor's heart. He died with his eyes open, according to Ockabunga who explained, "he had seen the truth."

The next day, the women and children of the tribe were invited to the feast of the white man. Ockabunga severed the head, then very excitedly explained to the rest of his tribe what was inside. They carefully opened a cavity in the back of the skull and scooped out the brains. They found no electricity, just a pink pulp which, when lightly fried in the fat of a wild pig, and sprinkled with jungle herbs, has an exquisite taste.

11. Leap of Faith

A United Nations bureaucrat loses his mind trying to find it

I don't know what year this is. The deconstructionists and post modernists long ago did away with the Julian calendar, claiming that it was an arbitrary way of structuring time forced on us by a white male dictator. Maybe so. But it has made life impossible for an old fashioned historian such as myself. If there is no officially accepted chronology, how can one write history? In fact, some historians I know have been fined for using the notations of "A.D." or "B.C." etc. Many refused to pay the penalty and ended up in gaol. But that's quite some time ago now. I can tell you though, I still use such words as "year" or "decade, " but they have little meaning to a young historian. The more timid historians of my generation will not even use the word "eon" which, because of its vagueness is sufficiently abstract to appeal to the deconstructionists who can make of it what they want. The far left deconstructionists even object to the very idea of history itself. They object to what they call the arbitrary division of time into past and future and insist that all prose be written in the present tense, even though they admit that logically the present cannot exist without reference to past and future. This is why all the documentaries on the History Channel use the present tense to describe events and people that occurred in the past.

The far right deconstructionists though, take the opposite view: that there should be no present tense in grammar because the present does not and cannot exist, because immediately an event occurs it has passed. It is present only for a split second, at the intersection between past and future, certainly not long enough to warrant writing about it in the present tense. Much of this ideological debate, of course, revolves around how one defines an "event." One can see that to go down that road would lead to an abyss of argument, to the infinite deconstruction of an event into its tiniest part. Unfortunately, it is the right wing deconstructionists who are dominant right now (they don't like that word of course), so I am not supposed to use the present tense at all. Anyway, I'm reaching the end of my life (both those words "end" and "life," arbitrary constructions in time, contend the left wingers, but acceptable so long as I acknowledge that the end of a life is but a beginning of another), so I intend to write my story any way I want. Though I hope that the reader will forgive any touches of sarcasm in my grammatically correct constructions here and there, which I sometimes cannot resist.

I have begun my very personal story with this digression because it's important that you understand the timeless wasteland in which I have lived and will live, and the place that appears to have existed and will exist for an eternity (a permissible word) where I have spent and will spend my working eternity at the United Nations Library and Documentation Center. My story begins (sorry, has begun and will begin) here.

*

Oh, but there is (was) just one other thing I should mention (have mentioned). This story cannot be written down for technical reasons that will become apparent as we get to the end of the story. It would be more accurate to say that I am telling (have told) the story without speaking it. It was in my head, and I have tried to get it out of my head and into yours. That is (was) all I can say/have said about it right now. Of course, there is also a practical reason why I have not and will not write this story down. It is seditious and would render me liable to a punishment of life without death. The story will begin now (shortly).

Just one other thing before I start. This was a true story and always will be.

For some time now (for a long time), I have known of a shadowy, mysterious figure who existed somewhere in the United Nations building basement (shadowy figures always skulk in basements). I say he existed because he has never been seen, though his presence is at times keenly felt by yours truly, and it has been surmised from the traces of his habitation in the bowels of the United Nations. I say somewhere even though I have gathered sufficient evidence to identify exactly where: it was the last office on the left, in the first level basement beneath the Great Hall of the General Assembly. Now I fully realize that "evidence" is the stuff that lawyers collect or social scientists accumulate to support their theories and that their critics always attack the methods used to collect such evidence. In my case, as an historian-come-anthropologist, I have dedicated my life to collecting only data from primary sources. I have done my best to be my own critic, not to fall into the common trap of "finding what I am looking for," as my critics sarcastically put it. But the evidence is the evidence. I must take it as it appears (sorry, appeared) and I certainly would never attempt to alter it or—far worse —invent it. That, of course, would be unforgivable fraud.

Self-deception I know is also a huge risk. Again, my critics point to my 'weakness" (I consider it my unique strength) of concocting a theory out of thin air. I say my theory is based on intuition, a talent I have for ferreting out the truth. All right, I know what you're thinking. I have done it all backward. I've made a few observations of "fact" then surmised a theory based on the observations. But all data are obtained through the senses are they not? Through observation preferably independent, preferably made at arm's length to avoid mixing up the process of observing with the data being observed. But there are other senses that we humans have besides seeing. As they say, seeing isn't always believing. But it is (was, will be) very close to it, in my opinion. OK. I have never seen Godfrey. But I have seen traces of his existence. He has left a trail of evidence. Isn't this typical of anyone? We leave (have left) traces of our presence (excuse me, our past and future!) no matter where we go or what we do. Any detective or CSI person will know (knows) that.

OK. I admit that I have never heard him speak either, though as we shall see, it depends on what one means by "heard." What I have experienced is a feeling of his presence. Like walking through someone's shadow. Call it a fifth sense, if you like. It's a physical sense I get on occasion when I'm in his office. And over the years I have spent a lot of time in his office. But I must have evidence that is more than just my own intuition, my fifth sense, do I not? Of course. I cannot expect anyone to believe me solely based on my own intuition. So what is (was) the evidence?

The evidence was (is) in the form of inscriptions hidden under layers of white acrylic paint. The first inscription that I uncovered begins (began) as follows:

THOU SHALT HAVE...

Only after fractions of eons of constant vigilance, taunted to breaking point by my fellow historians and document specialists at the United Nations, and having suffered the denial of promotion to Executive Historian because of my supposed "obsession," did I finally discover this first piece of tangible evidence. I had entered

Godfrey's office, carrying the latest batch of resolutions passed down from the General Assembly, when I noticed, as I raised the seat, that the paint had worn thin and there was the faintest trace of writing. I carefully placed the pile of documents (resolutions A/RES/66/1A through A/RES/66/285—the particular year of these resolutions has been erased from the records to conform with the administration's regulations) on the floor and kneeled down to get a closer look. I made out a "G" then tried to scratch off the paint to reveal the rest of the inscription. Unfortunately, in my excitement, I began poorly and lost some of the letters. But I was able clearly to make out a signature which read GOD in a tiny, cramped style, written with a fine felt-tipped pen. I copied the inscription on to the corner of one of the General Assembly documents and returned to my corner of the library (oops, I mean "documentation centre") to ponder my discovery.

"Well, not much of a discovery," you're saying (said, will say), "just a random piece of graffiti." Seemingly so. But there's the diff-erence between you and me. I have (had, will have) a nose for this sort of thing. I should have been a cold case detective, really. I knew that there was more from where this evidence came from. The problem was to find it, and I needed help to do it.

I first went to Lowes and Home Depot to sample all the kinds of paint stripper they had. The trouble was that it was too strong, did its job far too well. I wanted (want) only to remove one layer of paint at a time, not the whole damn lot. I set up a little lab at home and tried weakening the solutions, tried varying the pressure when I rubbed on the paint stripper, or the time I left the paint stripper sit on the surface. It was all just too chancy. I could not risk going (I am not sure whether this is grammatically correct, since "could" is past tense and "going" is present tense, is, was, it not?) to the research site and stripping away the evidence itself! There had to be another way.

For several weeks, I busied myself with the General Assembly resolution documents in my corner of the library. You may well ask, well why not do it in my office? And I am embarrassed to say that I do not (did not) have one. The fact was, some years ago (I am/was not permitted to say exactly how many years, let alone the word "years" for which I could, ironically, do a lot of "time" for using the word in this sentence) I was forced into retirement because I reached the U.N. mandatory retirement point—it used to be/was defined as the age (also a grammatically incorrect word) of sixty-two. But without the concept of years, sixty-two is meaningless. Anyway, my reaching the retirement point forced me out of my office. But I refused to retire and kept my U.N. staff ID, which they strangely never seriously asked me to give up. So nothing has really changed. I just keep/kept on turning up for work. My supervisor tolerated my presence provided I did not demand an office. Besides, U.N. staff move/d around a lot, and there is/was almost always a spare cubicle somewhere, which from time to time I ferret/ed out and used (and will use). But frankly, I preferred and will prefer my corner of the library. I have built high walls made of mounds of U.N. General Assembly documents to create a secluded corner. And there is no shortage of U.N. documents that arrive at a rate much faster than I can catalog. It is/was all I need/ed, and I have made a nice little spot for my old slippers that I will wear as soon as I will/have arrive/d in the library.

*

I made two decisions this morning. First, I am going to complete my story in a secret notebook away from prying eyes. I do not care if my notes are grammatically incorrect. I am fed up with the cumbersome grammar that results when one has no access to the present tense and must avoid the forbidden words of the Julian calendar. One cannot write with precision under such restrictions. Besides, I write, not for those deconstructionists and post modernists who dominate the present (a grand irony if ever there was one), but for those innocent souls whom I hope exist out there somewhere, who still understand the classical grammar of our forefathers, whose minds have not become besotted with the grammatical correctness of the postmodern era. At first, I thought that I should try to write in both deconstructive grammar and in classical mode, but as you no doubt have already seen in reading so far, the result is an impossible conglomeration of fractured words and abundance of parentheses.

The second decision I made was to send an email to INTERPOL's senior chemist Robert Etand, whom I met some years before on the second floor of the U.N. Library at the inaugural conference on the International Trafficking in Forbidden Words. He was the rapporteur, and I assisted him in writing the conference report (document A/386943b), almost impossible to draft without using those same forbidden words. So we kept in contact. My hope was that he could suggest how I could remove each layer of paint to reveal the inscriptions. To my amazement, he informed me that the simple solution was a little lemon juice or white vinegar. I preferred the lemon juice because of the smell of vinegar, which is not pleasant, especially in a library. I tried it at home, and it worked! I rushed to the office and went straight down to Godfrey's office and set about removing the first layer of paint. The result was the discovery of the three words I have just recounted. I was, naturally, overjoyed—only to be cruelly rebuffed by Godfrey's unpredictable ways. Try as I would with my lemon juice, it took six months to find any further inscriptions. I uncovered the next portion written inside a half inch band around the base of the wall, but the inscriptions were all of such indescribable obscenities, I dare not reproduce them here.

Further applications of lemon juice failed to reveal any more inscriptions until—I hesitate to say it, as I know few will believe me, but as an historian who takes his discipline seriously I am duty bound to report the facts—I had a dream in which I had the sensation of being suspended upside down while reading the next portion of Godfrey's inscriptions. I immediately woke up and wrote it out exactly:

... NO OTHER...

As soon as I had written it down, I rushed to the U. N. Plaza and down to Godfrey's office. My reasoning was that, if the dream was any indication of where the next portion of Godfrey's works could be found, it would be somewhere that requires one to suspend oneself upside-down, and the only place I could think of was under the seat. I applied my solution, and behold! There appeared a scrap of cramped writing, so tiny I needed a magnifying glass to read it. It was as clear as if it had been written yesterday:

...GODS BEFORE ME...

"Thou shalt have no other gods before me." Some may think it is strange that the very first inscription I uncovered turned out to be a commandment which has a very familiar ring to it. Be assured that I have spent hundreds of hours in the United Nations Information and Documentation Center and have uncovered no such commandment or one even vaguely similar to it in any U.N. documents. Others will accuse me of having made up the inscription, to which I can only reply that I am a responsible United Nations historian who takes his work too seriously to embark on such a reckless and irresponsible venture. It is true that, since Godfrey's grammatical constructions are often unnecessarily complicated and ponderous, I have taken the liberty, as the sole discoverer of these inscriptions, to simplify them and in so doing interpret them for the ordinary mind. It is a coincidence, though my critics would no doubt say that it is no coincidence, that the inscription is grammatically correct, avoiding the present tense and using the future. The criticism may well be raised that I should have, at the very outset, prepared a technical report for my fellow historians and superiors at the United Nations, rather than attempting immediately to popularize Godfrey's significant works. But I am sure that my peers are so blinded by their own set ways that they will not believe me. Over the years I have spoken to many of Godfrey's clients (some of whom are my colleagues and superiors) who must number in the thousands, people from an incredible array of races and cultures, from the furthest corners of the world. None of them remembers ever seeing Godfrey. I have probed with all my interviewing skills, pushed my respondents to the limits of their recall, but never have I found anyone who would admit to having seen him.

It was a challenge to my scholarship to establish the chronological (to hell with the regulations) order of Godfrey's inscriptions, and indeed, to separate one inscription from the other, especially when so many of them were embedded in a profusion of profanities. In anticipation of this problem, before uncovering more inscriptions, I spent many frenzied hours in the softly carpeted U. N. Information and Documentation Center studying the historical development of series documents, in particular, U.N. resolutions which number in the hundreds of thousands. This was a very puzzling problem of enormous import, and, speaking from a personal point of view (i.e., not as an historian), one that upsets me deeply each time I try to deal with it. I worry that the abolition of the Julian calendar was just the first step towards the abolition of numbers all together, since after all, the Julian calendar, or any calendar for that matter, depends on numbers to create order. Without numbers where would we be? I am sure that there is a postmodern deconstructionist working somewhere in the hidden library of Alexandria (the one in Egypt) with the sole intent of identifying the white male who invented the Arabic numerals just so they could be imposed on the rest of the world. I decided, therefore, in a fit of foolishness to count the U.N. documents to see how many there were in total. I now see what a truly stupid digression this was from my primary mission of finding references to the commandments I had uncovered. My emotional involvement in this problem became so great that I eventually took mouthfuls of tranquilizers before enter-ing the frescoed portals of the Information and Documentation Center, only to find that once I began my dizzy work of scouring and counting the documents, I would fall into a deep sleep.

I must now make a small confession of failure. Although I clung tenaciously to my task, in the end, I was forced to give it up. It was simply not humanly possible. After a full year's work, sometimes spending sixteen hours a day among the U. N. documents, I was able to read only a fraction of their holdings—at that rate, I could not have completed the task in my life(time). Worse, each time I fell asleep, I lost count and had to begin all over again when I woke up. Besides, I already knew that these holdings increased at a rate greater than I was able to count, let alone read them. No firm conclusions, therefore, could be drawn, and in the face of this failure, I withdrew to Godfrey's office in a fit of the severest depression. I must have stayed there days and nights. Occasionally well-meaning individuals would even offer me a cup of coffee, which I politely accepted. Then one morning—I think it was morning, though this is a guess because the only sources of light in the U.N. basement were fluorescent lights, there were no windows—my body suddenly shook in a spasm so violent that I fell off the seat. My head hit the hard, tiled floor, and I saw a big star explode. Something, a booming voice I think, literally "blew my mind," if you will excuse the coarse expression. I cannot claim that the voice spoke any particular words, although I am convinced that my understanding of whatever it said was that I was to rise up from my despair and attack it head-on. This is what I did.

In the months that followed, I worked eighteen hour days, rubbing off the white paint, copying down on expensive parchment paper every single word and letter. Everything. I searched all over New York till I found the fine felt-tipped pens that would allow me to reproduce exactly the cramped hand in which Godfrey had written his inscriptions. It also seemed that the more I applied my erasing solution, the more inscriptions appeared. I was hysterically happy, whistling as I worked, so much so that even some of Godfrey's old clients looked my way as they went by. Some, I think, even nodded "good day" to me.

It was not to last. After only a few months, having uncovered inscriptions on every inch of the cubicle's walls, I happened to press too hard on one point and erased the inscription. To my horror, another inscription was revealed underneath. I was incensed at this discovery. How could

Godfrey do this to me, having denied me for so long, suddenly to inundate me with his work? I felt cruelly taunted and began to wonder whether Godfrey was the benign and all revealing master craftsman I had arbitrarily (I admit this now) assumed him to be. He had placed me, the arch-historian, in the impossible position of having to destroy each inscription in order to discover another. Who could have believed that a dutiful historian such as I, who had devoted his whole career to making discoveries, should be so upset, even resentful at having made a new discovery? It was a situation I could not bear, and for the first time in hundreds of days, I removed myself from the United Nations and stayed at home. All this time I lay in bed eating only an occasional handful of breakfast cereal, keeping myself completely hidden under the covers.

Thank God that the spell was broken by a phone call from Robert Etand who had become a good friend over the years. The solution to my predicament was simple, according to Robert. He would take a series of photographs of each layer before I erased it. And if that were not enough, he would take infrared, and ultraviolet photographs which would demonstrate the existence of at least three layers of inscriptions. Further, he would sign an affidavit to the effect that the photographs were genuine. These assurances were sufficient to get me out of my bed and back to Godfrey's office. The photos turned out beautifully, but I suffer nevertheless the uneasy feeling that a picture of the inscription is not the actual inscription. I would have preferred to copy them all onto my parchment paper, a technique admittedly laborious, but surely producing a more authentic piece of work. Scholarship, after all, was not meant to be easy. But Robert, always the objective scientist, convinced me that if I wanted others to accept the validity of my discoveries, I must follow his path. Robert also solved the problem of chronology. He subjected each layer to a unique radio-active analysis and was able to establish unequivocally in which order the layers of paint had been applied. We discovered that each inscription was written on several levels. Godfrey typically began on a small square inch of the wall and built up the inscription through many layers. Thus, my first contact with each of Godfrey's command-ments (except the first) has been with their endings. I put together the fragments of eight more commandments, all of which have a familiar ring, yet none of which I was able to find any reference to in the United Nations Information and Documentation Center.

I became highly agitated, unable to concentrate on my work. I woke up screaming in the middle of the night. Yet I could never remember what the nightmare was about. I consulted once again with my good friend Robert Etand, who, as usual, was able to point to the solution. There had to be one more commandment, to make them up to ten which is, according to Robert, the perfect number. I rushed back to the office and applied more of my solution, even in little cracks and corners where I had never bothered to look before. Nothing appeared except a steady stream of obscenities. My nightmare began again, this time a little different not only because I could remember the details of each one, but worse because each night they became more and more violent. Then one night, the murder and mayhem of my dream became so dreadful I awoke screaming, "Thou Shalt Not Kill! Thou Shalt Not Kill!" And I knew as soon as I said it, that this was the missing inscription. I rushed into the office, as I had done many times before, and set to work. I looked under the seat, but there was nothing. The weeks and months (damn it, I do enjoy using these seditious words) went by, and I still could not find the missing commandment.

I turned once again to Robert for help. Once again he solved the problem instantly.

"Why are you still looking for the tenth commandment? You already have it, don't you?" he asked.

A strange calm took over me. Of course, he was right. I was so close to Godfrey that He had inscribed THOU SHALT NOT KILL directly into my brain! The search was over.

*

If only I could say that my story ended there. It's my own fault. No, no it's not. Not entirely, at least. It's in my nature to blame myself, but it can't be my fault if an event occurs that simply overshadows everything else. An event over which I had no control and that changed the course of history, my personal history, that is.

On the very day that I made my resolution to stop searching, I received a bomb threat. It was written in the same cramped hand of the Inscriptions. So I immediately knew who had made it. It fluttered under the door of Godfrey's cubicle where I was sitting, admiring the uncovered inscriptions, indulging in something of a reverie of self-satisfaction. The grammatically correct, though awkwardly written note said:

A BOMB WILL HAVE BEEN DEPOSITED

There are a number of bomb threats received by United Nations officials every week, and my superiors seem to know which threats are to be taken seriously, and which ones not. Without thinking, I went straight to my superior on the first floor to report the threat. He took the note and reacted without any concern at all. Naturally, I was distraught, because I feared that the bomb would destroy Godfrey's office, and I would never be able to prove his existence. I asked for the bomb threat back.

"Can't give it back to you. It's part of an official investigation now," said my superior.

"But sir, shouldn't I conduct the investigation? I know who wrote this note, I think," and immediately I said it, I wanted to take it back.

"You do?"

"Well, not exactly. But I recognize the handwriting."

"It's yours, isn't it? asked my superior, a smirk on his face.

"No, of course not, it doesn't look anything like my handwriting." I hesitated just a little, "at least I don't think so."

I looked down and began to back out of the office. My superior stared at me until I left. I could not understand why he did not have me detained if he thought I wrote the note. He seemed to think it was all a joke.

I returned to my corner of the library and put on my slippers. It was clear what I had to do. After the rebuff from my superior, I had no choice but to devote all my time to find out who had made the threat. I was suddenly transformed into an eager, aggressive invest-igator, from the quiet, withdrawn historian that I used to be.

My theory was that Godfrey knew I was close to discovering his identity, and he was trying to scare me off. I immediately dispatched a crisply worded memo to all my superiors and U. N. security officers, warning of an unknown terrorist in our midst. I placed a warning sign downstairs on level one, just outside Godfrey's office informing all Godfrey's clients that a bomb threat had been received in this very place.

They laughed at me. I was called up to the fortieth floor, a frightening experience. In all my many years as a U. N. civil servant, I had spent all my time on the level one basement and had never risen above the second floor. The chief security officer, the chief personnel officer and my immediate superior gave me a stern lecture. I was told that my imagination had run away with me. I was to stop issuing these warnings immediately. There were even threats, disguised as offers of help, to send me to a psychiatrist. I responded angrily, and, much to my regret, bragged that it was only a matter of days before I tracked down the terrorist. What made me especially able to do the work of the U. N. security service, for which I was not trained, they asked. And I replied, like a fool, that all the necessary leads were revealed in the Inscriptions.

They fell silent. My superior stepped forward and, very embarrassed, explained to the others that I had been searching for some mysterious inscriptions ("in his own time of course") for the last fraction of an eon (few years) which would throw important light on the early history of the United Nations.

They demanded to see the inscriptions. I refused. Was I not aware that they were U. N. property? Yes. Then was it not my duty to give them up? Yes. Then give them up. No! My superior, a gentle man and a consummate bureaucrat, suggested that we should adjourn the meeting, assuring the others that he would deal with the matter personally. It was agreed. The next day, I arrived at my usual corner of the library and discovered that my slippers were gone. I sat down on a pile of U.N. resolutions, put my head in my hands, and cried.

There was a rustling behind me. I turned to see my superior standing, holding my slippers out to me.

"These are yours, I think," he said.

I reached up to take them, but he pulled them back.

"Before I give them to you, we need to have a clear understanding," he said coldly.

I tried to stop crying and managed to reduce it to a whimper.

"I have not forgotten that you were retired from service long ago. I have let you run free. I have been very kind and tolerant of you. Now, you must do what I tell you, or we will both be destroyed." He waited for me to answer. But I did stop whimpering and looked up at him feeling like a little four-year-old.

I'm sending you on mission," he said, frowning, "to Rome, I'm sending you to Rome."

"But, but I'm retired," I complained.

"I know, I know. It's highly irregular. But I have managed to arrange it. Just sign these papers, and you will be on your way."

He handed me a sheaf of forms which I took.

"Why Rome?"

"I have a friend in the Vatican Library. He needs help."

"But, what about the terrorist?"

"Leave that to our security people."

"But all my work," I complained, indicating the mounds of documents that surrounded us."

"The Vatican Library is in a terrible mess. In order to comply with U.N. GA Resolution 8974B, they have been trying to revise all their old documents to replace all forbidden words with the correct ones. I think you're just the man to help them, given your experience with all this." He gestured to the waist high piles of documents.

"But the bomb threat. It's more urgent," I pleaded.

"You're going to Rome, and that's that. If you do not, I'll ask you for your U.N. ID, and you will no longer be able to enter this building. Your choice."

The events of those few days, as I prepared to take my leave, were utterly devastating. Blinded by my superior's lack of concern over the bomb threat, I did not realize, almost until too late, what Godfrey was up to. For, as I sorted out Godfrey's inscriptions in preparation for my departure, I immediately saw that I had been so engrossed in learning all about Godfrey and His works, that I had not given the slightest consideration to the quite reasonable response on his part: that over the fraction of eons I had studied him, he had studied me. This sudden realization sent my mind reeling back to the first encounters I ever had with Godfrey, which for obvious reasons, I have kept secret all this time.

You see, I have personally known Godfrey for many years. I encountered him on the very first day I took up my post as Assistant Historian to the Undersecretary, Division of Economic and Social Grammar. At that time, it had been my intention to join the fight against World Hunger. The beautiful delegate from Ethiopia had just taken the floor of the General Assembly, and I had suddenly felt a prickly feeling around my collar, due to a hot flush that had overtaken my whole face and neck. I excused myself.

On looking back, I now realize that I must have been ill because I behaved in a most disorganized manner, which is simply not like me. I found myself running out of the Great Hall, my hand pulling at my silk neck tie and shirt collar, responding to a sensation of being grabbed or squeezed around the neck. I wanted to throw up, yet instead of going to the nearest bathroom which is situated just outside the door of the Great Hall, I found myself stumbling down the escalator to the lower level, ending up in what I now know as Godfrey's office. I was surrounded by travel brochures and books—the cubicle was lined from top to bottom with them. The memory of them is so clear that I know I could not have been mistaken. I can even tell you the titles and colours of many of them, because I was there, throwing up, gasping for air for a long time, and as often happens, when one is in such a condition, a thoroughly detailed photograph etched itself on my memory. In fact, the memory is so vivid, I wish it would go away. A night in bed never passes without the picture of Godfrey's shelves of travel books flashing into my eyes.

I have been back to Godfrey's office three times a day ever since, and that includes weekends, but each time, Godfrey must have heard my approach and cunningly turned down the OCCUPIED latch. Or, if I did manage to catch him unawares, he managed —don't ask me how—to clear all his travel books out, and the walls which I would examine carefully, would be freshly painted, leaving no trace of the book shelves.

His travel books led me astray for some time, because I foolishly thought that if I could somehow reconstruct his office the way I first found it, with the same travel books on the same shelves, Godfrey would be enticed out of hiding, and I would at least get to meet him face to face. I, therefore, searched the catalogs of the United Nations Information and Documentation Center for the brightly bound travel books that I well-remembered but found no such books.

And I could (can) smell him. It was a sweet and pungent odour of cologne, a type of cologne I have tried to identify without success. I have collected so far 5,302 bottles of cologne from all over the world, had them analysed by my good friend Robert Etand of INTERPOL. None fits the samples of air I have collected from Godfrey's office.

When my superior came by Godfrey's office (as everyone inevitably must), I tried to explain to him that I was on the verge of a great discovery, that it would be wrong to send me to Rome; that I had at last uncovered the logic or the motive underlying Godfrey's actions. My superior very bluntly pointed out to me that I had spent fifteen years (he even used that seditious grammar) searching for Godfrey, wasn't it time I gave it up? He had me cornered. The situation was simply too much for me. I rushed into Godfrey's office, gathered up an armful of Godfrey's inscriptions, and tossed them at my superior's feet, feeling as though I had thrown down the gauntlet, or something like that. He looked at me, not a trace of interest or even any emotion on his face; didn't even ask me what they were; just turned to look in the mirror. Like Pilate, he washed his hands and muttered, "you will go to Rome."

I have never struck anyone in my life before, never raised my hand, even to an animal, but I confess that I would have crashed my tight fist into the back of my superior's neck, I was so angry. Instead, Godfrey intervened. Yes, Godfrey. He appeared in the mirror looking out over my superior's shoulder. I can remember a few details of his face—an old face, covered with silver stubble, smooth puffy cheeks, a heavily lined forehead, huge ears, and a toothless grin. It was a grin not meant for amusement, but rather to mock me, which precisely fitted my new interpretation of Godfrey. The travel books, the perfumes, the mixed-up stories, the layers of inscriptions and all the other challenges that I had grappled with for fifteen years: Godfrey had been playing with me, mocking me. My anger was immediately transformed into a keen sense of resentment; a feeling that I must repay Godfrey on his own terms. Godfrey's image disappeared, and I found myself smiling to my superior, offering him a soft towel, agreeing that I must go to Rome. If my suspicions were correct, God- frey would follow me there.

*

My first order of business upon arriving in Rome was to purchase an extremely accurate chronometer, one that could tell me within one second, the exact time in New York City. This was not an easy matter. Un-deconstructed time pieces were scarce since most watches and clocks of the traditional variety had been destroyed by the deconstructionists along with their terminology. A deconstructed time piece had only one hand, and the face was divided into two halves, one for night, the other for day. LED time pieces that showed numbers were forbidden. My friend Robert from INTERPOL had advised me where to get one in Rome. I was to go to the central train station where the illegal North Africans sold all kinds of forbidden items in the narrow alleys behind the station. The train from the airport dropped me off right there. I stepped out into the street, and there were African vendors everywhere openly selling their illegal wares. I chose a handsome Rolex and paid just $5 for it, knowing of course that it may or may not have been the real thing. Either way, it was an illegal time piece that was a significant risk to anyone who kept it on their person, punishable by several fractions of an eon in prison.

I was soon on my way to the great church of St. Peters, carrying a little leather handbag in which I had carefully placed my Rolex, a small bottle of lemon juice, and a powerful magnifying glass. When I arrived at the church, I immediately descended into the crypt under the Bernini altar. Here, on the walls of the narrow passageways that connect to the popes' tombs, I knew that many old frescoes had been neglected by the experts because they were second-rate. I chose the flesh colour of an angel's figure and began rubbing gently with my lemon juice. Nothing. Which is what I expected. I looked over my shoulder, expecting to be accosted, but the tourists took no notice of my furtive doings. I rubbed a little more, this time turning my attention to the darker tints. Still nothing. "Perhaps the halo," I thought with a smile, thinking this would be enough to flush Godfrey out. I rubbed some more, but nothing except a few tiny specks of dark blue. I rummaged in my bag for the magnifying glass and raised it to my eyes. And then I knew he was behind me.

A man was shaking my elbow and yelling at me in Italian. I dropped the magnifying glass and ran back up into the church, heading straight for the stairs that led to the top of the massive dome of Michelangelo. The man followed me, as I had expected, indeed, as I had planned. I looked at my Rolex and smiled as I ran up the marble steps taking them three at a time. My pursuer followed, but I kept just enough ahead of him so that he could not quite catch me, yet was too close to give up the chase. We came to the balcony around the middle of the dome. I ran to one side, looking down over the lower railing, the curved dome above and the distance to the floor below making me giddy. I stepped back quickly as my assailant lunged towards me, then I pretended to trip and fall backward. He lost his balance and fell forward, grabbing my shoulders with both hands. My feet left the marble floor. His weight pushed down on my chest. We were balanced over the railing, my back almost splitting in two. For a second we were balanced like a see-saw. I tried to kick my legs forward, but gravity (it was Godfrey really) was too strong. Slowly we tipped (were tipping) over, my assailant dissolving away and I fell (was falling), staring up at the magnificent dome, the blinding light of faith blasting down from its centre, its rectangular frescoes spinning around me, then rapidly receding as I dropped past the inscription that said REGNI CAELORUM and then I knew that Godfrey was no threat, but a promise of the vast light from above.

12. Civilization

A tribe of cannibals begins the path to civilization

One can readily understand the feelings of revulsion and disgust we felt upon hearing how Ockabunga killed and ate his friend, Doctor Lewis Berger. Indeed, that is how I felt as a long-time friend and student of the great Doctor. But as an anthropologist trained in Doctor Berger's tradition, I must try to see the event from the point of view of Folijot culture, which leads me to conclude that to kill and eat his friend was, for Ockabunga, the supreme act of love; the climax to an intensely intimate relationship. One might even put it in Western terms by saying that Ockabunga took Doctor Berger "into his bosom." Admittedly, this is a little farfetched because in Western Culture the saying is meant to be symbolic, whereas in Folijot culture the "taking in" is actual.

I anticipate that this observation leaves me open to the charge that I am judging Folijot Culture as "less developed" than Western Culture in the sense that the Folijot are unable to separate the symbolic from the real. I hasten to reply that indeed I consider that they have not made this distinction, but that there is absolutely no basis whatever to claim that the splitting of these two, as has occurred in Western Culture, is either "progress" or desirable. The trouble in Western Culture—and many theorists as well as myself have noted this—is that we have lost contact with the core roots of our existence, the granite of our natures, that our lives have become too abstract, devoid of real meaning. This is the source of our alienation, dis-ease, unhappiness.

One need spend only an hour talking with Ockabunga to see the truth in this assertion. The simplicity with which he sees the world, the clarity of his mind, the almost clairvoyant look in his eyes. He and his fellow warriors suffer no complexes, alienations, guilt. They live at one with nature and each other. The fact that they happen to be head-hunters and cannibals is mostly incidental. In fact, I would argue that in many ways their cannibalism has a most positive effect on their culture. It keeps them tied to the concrete, real meaning of existence which is the cycle of life and death: by eating the corpse, they gain sustenance from death. Life in this sense is brought into direct dependence on death, so that there is no impossible duality between Eros and Thanatos as there is in Western Culture, where we are so infantile in our denial of death, to the point that we deny life as well.

When I first followed Ockabunga to his straw hut, the one in which he and Doctor Berger had lain together for almost three years, my mind was overcome by the terrible anticipation of seeing Doctor Berger's preserved head. In fact, I almost withdrew from the entire expedition because I was so frightened that I would lose control of myself. My mind buzzed with all the possible things that my body could do to me. I might vomit uncontrollably; I might cry; I might attack and kill Ockabunga; or I might direct the soldiers, who were accompanying me, to kill him. I knew, as an anthropologist, that I must not do any of these things.

"Sit down," said Ockabunga, and I dropped cross-legged onto the straw mat outside the hut; the exact place where I imagined Doctor Berger had reposed many times.

"Thank you," I said, looking around for the Doctor's head among the others that hung down from the eaves of the hut by thin strands of hair.

"Doctor Berger was my good friend!" grinned Ockabunga, rolling his eyes.

"He was my excellent friend also."

"He teach me very much."

"He taught me a lot too."

"He teach anatomy, but not understand."

"Why not?"

"We try. Nothing there. No electricity."

"I don't understand."

Ockabunga went into his hut and returned with the dried out recognizable head of Doctor Berger. He threw the head to me, forcing me to catch it. To my surprise, instead of reacting with tremor, I was instead fascinated and suffered a compulsion to rub my hands lightly over and over the surface of the Doctor's head. Over and over, I turned it around and around in my hands, feeling the eye sockets, the hard shiny surface. There was something about the touch of it that I couldn't help liking. Saliva even started to run in my mouth, although I was certainly not hungry.

"You see, we make hole, take out brains, no electricity." Ockabunga reached forward to take the head from me to show where he had opened the cranium. But I wouldn't, couldn't, let it go; had to keep rubbing it. Ockabunga then reached for his spear, and I suddenly came to my senses and dropped the head as though it had become quite hot. He examined the point of his spear.

"This spear kill good Doctor here," Ockabunga grinned as he pressed his index finger to my chest. I smiled and had to fight the notion that slipped into my mind: that this guy was a goddamned Primitive Savage! A heretical thought I know! But I confess it in order to make known the terrible temptations to which we scientists are sometimes subjected. One of the soldiers stepped forward menacingly. I let him stay there.

Although I'd learned a lot from Doctor Berger, I've learned a lot more by myself. It's one thing to love these beautiful natives, but it's another to be permissive and protective of them. I wasn't going to let this guy boss me around like he had Berger because the fact of the matter is that I have worked out an unassailable position as regards these different cultures. If you subscribe to the view of the cultural relativists—pioneered by the great Doctor Berger, and now largely adopted worldwide in modern anthropology—it follows that the only thing that counts is how powerful one culture is against another. For example, the Folijot Warriors feast mainly on another neighbouring weaker culture; they take it for granted, both the Folijot and the tribe whose members they eat. It's a concrete fact of nature if you understand me. It follows, therefore, that if my culture is stronger, it's only natural that it takes over the Folijot. This is why I came on this expedition with soldiers. It may well be that the Folijot, once very happy, will become unhappy now that they have been brought into contact with the West. This is not to say that the influence of the West is "bad." It is simply to note the facts of relativism: one's happiness can only be evaluated relative to another. And it is the one whose interests dominate who will be happiest.

It might be argued that this will lead to the destruction of Folijot culture. That may well be so. But who are we as scientists to interfere with the inevitable march of history? To do so is to play God. Dr. Berger in many ways played God by protecting the tribes he discovered because he dared to decide which culture should survive and which one not, while all the time claiming that every culture was as "good" as any other. He was, however, a weak God and suffered a weak God's very ancient fate. I, on the other hand, am a purist. I am determined to allow all events to play themselves out. We must not impose our values on history, and as well, science is a part of history and must be allowed to take its place.

The grant that I received from the A.I.C.F. (American Inter-Cultural Foundation) was substantial. It will allow me to study these natives in far greater depth, and with much greater precision than was ever possible. And, because it will be an open study, my data, in contrast to Doctor Berger's, will be verifiable. Briefly, the research design is as follows.

First, my research assistants will live among the Folijot, participating in head hunting and eating human flesh. We consider this to be absolutely necessary as a preliminary exercise so that we are sure we understand the content of Folijot culture fully. The field workers will then interview (using, of course, a standardised structured schedule) those whose heads are about to be severed, to obtain their attitudes to life and death.

Next, comes the most crucial and innovative step in the research. We will randomly assign members of the tribe into two groups: one group, the control, we will leave alone. The other group, after we have interviewed their potential victims, we will instead provide the potential victim with the opportunity to kill his assailant. (The exact method has not been adequately worked out. We would prefer a gun, which would do the job quickly and cleanly, but the problem with this is that the victims would have to be selected in advance and taught to use the gun, thus introducing an extraneous factor into our carefully controlled research design). Then we will immediately interview the would-be assailant as to his attitudes to life and death. One can see that this experimental intervention creates a situation of crisis which we consider to be very conducive to interview response depth. We have termed it the "generative crisis technique." After the "victim" has killed his "assailant," we will then re-interview him to check whether his attitudes to life and death have changed. One can see that the research design is quite complicated, but very rigorous, and, most important, achieves a blend of two heretofore competing approaches to research: the experimental method is applied in a real life setting.

It will be seen that an experimental intervention is also an attempt (unashamedly, I might add) to introduce a distinct change in the dynamic structure of Folijot society. It introduces the notion of reciprocity—that is, if you kill someone else, you must expect to be killed in return. The Folijot, while remaining warriors, become no longer predators, but rather kill with the expectation of being killed.

Thus we have introduced the rudiments of a just society.

13. Deconstruction

A master lectures his apprentice on truth

Once upon a time a cook, who was getting old and was a little hard of hearing, was preparing a salad. He reached for an orange and was about to slice it, when his bright young apprentice asked, "what's the orange for?"

"What's an orange?" replied the cook, "what kind of question is that?"

"I said, 'what's it for,' not what is it. But come to think of it, what is an orange anyway?" the apprentice asked cheekily.

"You want to know what an orange is? Here, I'll show you."

The cook sliced it in two, and it so happened that one of the parts was much bigger than the other. He proceeded to slice the large piece into three pieces, and the other into two.

"What have you discovered?" asked the apprentice, noting the obvious satisfaction the cook showed by his accomplishment.

"I now know not only what this orange is, but also, the larger piece tells me much more about the orange than the other pieces combined."

"But aren't they all the same?" asked the apprentice.

"Don't be foolish, haven't you got eyes?" the cook replied scornfully, "can't you see that each of the five parts is clearly of a different size and that the larger part has all those little pips? And you know what those pips will turn into, don't you?"

"An orange?" asked the apprentice querulously, stating what he thought was obvious, annoyed that he was spoken to as if a four-year-old.

"Very good!"

The cook stepped out to receive a delivery from the grocery store. The puzzled apprentice immediately placed himself in front of the orange. He reached for a piece of butcher's string and began to tie the pieces of the orange together in order to make it whole again. It was an impossible task because the pieces of orange would not stay in place. Each time he tried to tighten the string around them. It kept slipping off, and the pieces fell apart. The apprentice stopped and thought very hard, so hard, his head ached. But it was worth the effort because very soon a great idea struck him: Perhaps the pieces could be tied together more easily into a different shape? Indeed, this turned out to be the case, and he was able to tie all the pieces back to back so that the skin faced the inside, and the flesh, the outside. He sat in front of his masterpiece, beaming with pride.

The cook returned. "What are you doing?" he growled.

The apprentice quivered. "I thought I'd try to join the pieces together, and in that way, I could tell much more about the orange than just one large piece on its own. And besides, we can now see inside the orange and at the same time keep it whole."

"That's ridiculous! It's obvious that the pieces will not go back together. I thought you were smarter than that!"

The apprentice cringed as his master continued.

"What's the point of putting the pieces of an orange back together again? If that were important, I wouldn't have cut it up in the first place, would I?"

"I don't know, master," answered the apprentice.

14. Fake Truth

A political activist speaks from his basement bedroom

I sleep until midday, when my iPhone 11X awakens me and plays, from my new Sirius subscription, the beeps of the BBC world news. They still haven't left the EU and Johnson still blabbers with his foul English American accent. I switch to my Rush Limbaugh subscription to hear the latest lies and distortions of the Great Leader of the left. I roll out of my single bed, the sleeping bag falls bunched up on the floor, stuffing pushing out through holes that I have worn from constant rubbing of my legs and feet. It's my allergies. I have hives, or maybe it's eczema. The itching drives me crazy. I can't go to a doctor, because I don't have health insurance and my shitty parents will not pay for me anymore. And they let out my bedroom to some student who says she wants to be a nurse. She's hardly ever there. Works most nights and at school in the day, says she has to pay for her keep somehow or other. Stupid bitch doesn't understand how she is abused and exploited by the ruling class. They rule you by debt. If my parents knew what was good for them they'd let me have my bedroom back again. The air in this basement is humid, and smells of mould. One day, they'll pay for their ignorance. It's a day I look forward to. And it won't be long now.

At least they let me have a TV and use their cable. I don't think they know I use their account. I'm expecting them to cut it off any day. Just because they think I'm one the masked ANTIFA crowd. Well I'm not. I don't go out except to buy a few things at the ACME supermarket. Cuomo is on CNN. They're going to get Trump this time, so they say. It won't happen. The ruling class will see to that. Unless he becomes too much of an embarrassment. Then they'll purloin his riches and put him in prison. And I know how they'll do it. I worked for the FBI one time, was a special agent. So why am I stuck in my parents' basement, masturbating and eating bags of baked lentil chips? Well I'm not polluting the environment am I? I was— still am—a CIA operative too. Very low level, which is where I prefer.

I send them important information I get from my cunning infiltration of the right wing web sites and the corporations that espouse capitalist trickle down nonsense.

I flip to MSNBC. Chris Matthews is on. What a great icon of the left! A true old fashioned democrat. Always speaks our truth. But he sits there, talking too fast, splattering spit on his guests who take it with a smile. He's too old. I could do his job. I know a lot more than he does. And besides he thinks he speaks the truth but he doesn't know what's true and what isn't. What was true in his day is no longer true today.

Take for instance the blog I'm writing right now for my daily lesson on real political theory on my blog site:

www.policaltruthisnotfake.com

Here is what I have written so far. I always begin with the same sentence.

I am the truthsayer.

Everyone knows that Marx was a Jew. He wasn't. Well, he was, but then he wasn't. You can find evidence all throughout his writings. His description in *Das Capital* of the tailor making clothes, the prototype he claimed as the foundation of capitalism, the exploitation of labour. He obviously had a Jew in mind. The Shylock who extracted his pound of flesh or more from his workers. And for what end? Simply to accumulate money. The Jews, that's what they did, and that's what they do now. They hoard money. And what about Marx's widely acknowledged essay "On the Jewish Question?" What more evidence could you want?

The fact is, according to my careful research of his life in New York when he was reporting on the American Civil war for *The New York Times,* in 1862, he was turned. That's right. Turned, just like an ISIS acolyte. But it was his close friendship with Archbishop John Hughes that turned him into a Roman Catholic. And Marx saw to it that Hughes established the many communist catholic charities throughout New York City. How else can one explain the rampant promotion of capitalism by the great protestants of America? They rose up against the threat of Roman Catholic Communism, which has continued its spread until this very day. The Roman Catholic Church is now ruled by Pope Francis, an obvious communist embedded in the violent communist politics of South America, and of course, a Jesuit, all of whom are essentially Marxist worshippers.

Marx received a special dispensation from Archbishop Hughes that freed him from having to worship Jesus openly nor go to church. He had his own small chapel hidden in his bedroom which he shared with no one, except his housemaid, who he screwed from time to time. Engels' letters refer to those trysts as such. It is what led Marx to move to England, followed shortly by Engels. Their relationship remained tense. It is why Engels wrote his book, *The Conditions of the Working Class in England*, without Marx as co-author.

I know what you're thinking. That famous saying by Marx in his On the Jewish Question, that religion is the opiate of the masses. That does not mean that he disapproved, not at all. He did, in fact, partake of his own opiate, cocaine in particular. Archbishop Hughes probably took advantage of that weakness of Marx to turn him into a Roman Catholic of the most secret kind.

So say, I, the Truthslayer.

I always end with that. No. It's not a typo. Mao said, "To build you must first destroy," (No he didn't, though he could have). He was wrong though. Power doesn't come from the barrel of a gun. It comes from destroying words and replacing them with their opposites.

15. Secret of the Sand

A scientist discovers a secret of nature that he cannot reveal

I truly miss the beach, the open stretches of wet sand, the rolling surf, the undulating dunes covered with spine grass and tea-tree. The memories of my childhood beach days are sensuous to the point of torment: the sand sticking to my legs; the taste of sea salt on my lips; the cold of the water as a wave breaks over my head. After a vigorous swim, my friends and I used to roll down the dunes, then lie on our bellies soaking up the heat of the sand. Ah, such memories!

The day I returned to my beach, I regretted having left it, because it just wasn't the same. No, I mean it was the same, too much like I remembered it, the dunes, the grass; but it was I who was not the same. And I was alone as never before. I climbed atop the biggest dune—our dune—at a secluded spot along the Great Ocean Road— and contemplated the roll to the bottom.

Of course, I only contemplated it. It's what kids do, not adults who have a wife and family. Instead, I sat on the sand for a long time with my legs tucked up under my arms, stuck to the dune like one of the big red rocks that lay strewn along the beach. I was in a kind of daze, the sun beating down on the back of my neck. But there was one thing that I could do that we all did when no one was looking, I could have a pee under the nearby tea-tree. There, I dropped down on both knees and directed a stream in a forward arc, the liquid, trickling around the contours of the sand. It was when I was just expunging the last drops that I became aware of—there are no other words to describe it— aware of a Presence.

I should say that I am embarrassed at using such terminology. It sounds so transcendental, so religious, and for an accomplished bio- logist such as I am, there is no place for such language. But I cannot deny that this is what I felt, and there is no choice but to use such words to describe my experience. This is not to say, of course, that this and other similar experiences cannot be described in scientific terms. Certain anthropologists and biologists would describe such an experience as "a primitive archetypal reaction" to, say, the stark shadows cast by the bushes, or perhaps to particular combinations of rustling sounds.

All I could see around me, as I hastily zipped myself up, were the gently swaying tea-tree bushes and their latticed shadows on the sand. I heard the crackling of twigs as if someone were treading lightly beneath the bush. Then nothing. I walked up over the dune, down into a little gully that opened out on the flat of the beach, where the waves, having spent their power, ebbed across the sand, in some places smoothing it, in others where small gusts of wind zipped around the rocks, imprinting the sand with their ripples. I felt like I was following someone, although I could see no one; see no footprints.

The wind blew across the surface of a tiny pool that had been trapped behind a ridge of sand. I looked in, and there I saw the shadow of Adam (the name just popped into my head), at first barely discernible against the reflection of the sky, then slowly, shakily, appearing. It was the picture of a person so beautiful as to be indescribable. The image suddenly shortened and was gone, and I turned around to see that Adam had squatted down on his haunches. He smiled at me, and I saw the smiles of my daughter when she was two years old. His hand came out to touch my hot cheek, and I felt my mother's hand of many years ago. He sat back, stretching out his legs, and I remembered my friends on the dune.

"What is your species?" I asked foolishly. But he did not reply, merely beckoned me to come closer, to sit beside him.

I did not, for to do so, I would not have been able to look at him in the way I wanted. I would have been too close to him, and anyway I admit that I was afraid to touch him.

Perhaps my eyes were playing tricks on me? A little sunstroke, maybe? I scooped a little water out of the pool and patted it on my forehead and the back of my neck. Some more for my eyes. Perhaps when I opened them, he would be gone.

He remained. We looked at each other. I know it seems strange, but I could not make out the details of his physical form, yet he was so clearly there, his dark glistening skin against the glare of the sky and sand. He was there alright.

"Where are you from?" I asked, but he replied only by rolling over onto his belly, his buttocks and hips protruding like a woman's. The sand, not just granules but on mass, adhered to his body like a viscous fluid.

I had the urge to dig my open fingers straight into him as one does when digging into the sand. But I was still too frightened to touch him. I squatted down, my bottom dipping into the pool.

"What do you want?" I asked, my fear translating into the aggression of my species.

Again, he merely smiled, reminding me of all the daughters I have known, then rolled back onto his side, the mass of sand clinging to his breasts so much so that I could not discern where his breasts and the sand parted. Adam propped his head on his elbow, and with the other arm, he beckoned me closer. The arm, a deep dark brown, glistening with oil, reached right to me, stroking me lightly behind the ear, the index finger following the line of my jaw to my chin. I shuffled a little closer. Then, surprising myself, I found I was leaning forward on all fours trying to focus my eyes on that part of his body that seemed to be—well, I hate to say this— non-existent. What I mean is that I think—no, I can be more definite than this—I know that his body was completely nude, yet I was unable to discern his gender, which was blotted out like they do on TV. And, yes, I know what I have told you so far has been misleading. I assumed that Adam was a "he" when he could well be a "she." It doesn't really matter. Anyway, it makes it very clumsy if I have to write "he/she" and so on. Rather I have used "he" as in "He" just as we do not write "god," but we do write "God."

I was seized again with this great urge to thrust my hand into Him. A scientist should, after all, check out something that at first seems very strange to him, and usually, he will find some simple explanation. But I was worried that if I gave into my urge, if I jumped right in there, so to speak, I might destroy what I was trying to study. I, therefore, kept the lid on my desire, as every good scientist must.

Adam may have guessed what I was thinking. Ever so slightly, He pushed his hips towards me. It was an unmistakable invitation, but I resisted.

"How old are you?" I asked, brashly.

Adam's smile vanished. He frowned, yet I could see no lines on his face. I was feeling rather than seeing. "This guy hasn't lived," I thought to myself, regaining my scientific composure. For now, I realized that I had before me the most incredible biological find of the century. This was an unknown species, an abominable sand man! I took out my notebook and pencil and expanding rule, which I always carry because a biologist never knows when he will come across a notable specimen.

"Can you talk?" I asked, pointing at his mouth, putting a finger to my throat.

He no longer responded with his beautiful smile. Instead, His face had become hard, sullen. By now I didn't care about His lovely smiles. He was a great find, and I was determined to put it all down on record. I opened up my measure and placed it around His head, then made a series of measurements over the whole of His body, recording them all carefully in my notebook. He wouldn't move, though, so I had to make do with taking all the measurements with Him lying on his side. And it seemed that with each measurement I took, His body became harder and stiffer, and it lost its shiny, oily surface. In fact, when I ran the measure down to his legs, I distinctly felt His skin become rough as sand, the leg as hard as a rock. I say "seemed," quite aware that scientists do not like the use of such vocabulary, because I must, as a scientist, also be honest. The truth of the matter is that I had become so hot with this frenzied activity of measuring and recording, the sun beating down on my neck, that I was quite dizzy toward the end, unsure of exactly what I was doing. In fact, as I was about to make the last set of measurements that would have required placing one end of the measurement at Adam's crotch, I was seized with such a feeling of exhaustion, that I threw down my measure, my notebook and pencil, tore off my clothes and rushed for the surf.

The first big wave knocked me under the water, and the chill of the sea brought sense back into my head. What had I done? I had run away from the find of the century merely because I was a little hot and wanted a swim! I rushed out of the water and across the ribbed sand to the gully. Adam was gone, as I fully expected. Not a trace of Him was left in the sand. Not the slightest feeling of His Presence. I looked around for my notebook and pencil and found them floating in the little pool. Thank God! The records I had made were still legible, though very faint. I have since gone over them all very carefully in an indelible pen that the makers guarantee will never fade.

There is a drawer in my closet that contains a lot of old clothes that I never wear. I keep my notebook there, hidden under an old woollen sweater. When I'm home alone, when my kids are away at school, and my wife is out shopping, I go to the drawer and retrieve it. I open it and look at the indelible scratchings. I cannot believe that I wrote those notes. In fact, when I read them, they make no sense to me. I must have been out of my mind, plainly delusional, stricken by the sun. On a number of occasions, I have even thrown the book in the trash, only to retrieve it soon after.

How could I tell anyone of my discovery, or, should I say, "experience" described in my notebook? If anyone in my office read it, I'd be fired on the spot. And how embarrassed I would be if my wife and kids saw it. What would I say? How could I explain it? My family has a father who suffers from delusions? Weird jottings of a slightly deranged mind? I don't know how I could have been so foolish to write down, put into words, what I saw that day. I had a silly idea that simply by recording my experience in a notebook that this was "evidence," that what I saw was real. Instead, it made the whole event unreal, because no one could ever believe what I wrote. Instead, they would say that what I wrote was not an accurate description of what I saw, but was merely ramblings of a sunstroke victim. And why not? I can't believe it myself, except that I know what I saw and felt, and to me it was real.

Today I turned 65, and technically I'm eligible for social security. I can't live with my secret any longer, so I have bought a shredder, and I'm going to shred it and throw it in the trash. My family will never know. There will be no "evidence" left behind when I die. And as I feed each page into the shredder (a cross cut shredder I should add) I try to forget the beach and the sun and the sand. And the memory will fade and become no more.

It's early morning, and I am sitting in our living room looking out over our front garden, sipping a cup of Starbucks. We are on the brink of winter, and the lawn and withered flower beds are receiving the soft flakes of our first snow. I couldn't sleep at all last night. I kept going over and over what was in the notebook. It has become an obsession that will not go away. I have reached the point where I am desperate to tell someone. But if I do, what then?

16. Mixed Blessings

Men, together, at the stainless wall.

A shiny wall of metal
Beckons.
Three men step up.
One tall, one short, one wide,
Hands unseen,
Rubbing shoulders,
Touching, gently stroking
Names, endless names.
They look, eyes closed,
Heads bowed.
Streams of life forced down
Strands entwined
As they trickle away
As one.

17. Rounding Error

A society gets off on the wrong foot and is saved by hypocrisy

"The Klinger Round was created by Doctor Klinger when he was only twenty-six, his first year out of medical college. Such dexterity, imagination, feeling, all combined in one man," whispered the Intern, as a group of admiring students watched the Doctor slowly unwrap the coils of shiny white silk. Doctor Klinger had always insisted upon pure silk vestments regardless of cost. "Taste and Trust go together," was his favourite saying.

The Intern continued. "Doctor Klinger has always insisted upon unwrapping the silks himself. A doctor must maintain a close personal relationship with his patient, as he expounds in his recent book, The Doctor, and Your Self. Honours students should pay particular attention to the chapter on the symbolic interpretation of vestments in all aspects of salving as well as with the Round which you see today."

The Intern stopped, sniffed in quickly through dilated nostrils, and ran her eyes over her group of students. She could see that they had not listened to a word she had said, they were so entranced by the Doctor. She didn't mind at all. It was an honour to be there with him and to see this bright group of students drinking in his teachings.

Doctor Klinger deftly twisted the streams of silk with an arcing movement of the right arm, winding up the slack with a supple flick of the left hand. It was evident to all that this man knew what he was doing. He never faltered. The Intern had watched him countless times. Always, he did it in the same way, standing in the same posture, long legs astride, head and shoulders arched forward like a Spanish bull, head cocked to one side while he spoke soothingly to his patient. Occasionally he would stop, running his hands lightly over the silk strands, enjoying the smooth feeling on his fingers.

"How are you feeling, Constance?" asked the Doctor, displaying his remarkably clipped accent, the envy of those who yearned for higher social positions.

"I'm so excited Doctor. I don't know what to say. But John Peters is he...?"

"Not now, my dear, tell us a little more about how you feel," probed the good Doctor. He had written many papers on the mentally elevated state of Rounding patients when they experienced their Round. He wanted the students to see it first-hand.

"I'm-I'm just in love with the world," smiled Constance, adding a little giggle, "I mean, I'm sort of glowing inside, as though I were conceiving, pregnant, and giving birth all at once!" she blurted. The students shuffled, and there was the dull rustle of pencils to paper. Doctor Klinger smiled ever so faintly, knowingly.

"It's so overwhelming," Constance continued, "it seems as though a force or something is operating, much greater than any of us can imagine. It's ... well…" she hesitated and bit her bottom lip, "—it's divine!" She blushed and turned her head away from the fascinated student audience, trying to hide her face in the pillow. Her dark hair fell in waves across her cheeks as she placed her forearm across her eyes.

The Intern caught the attention of her students with a quick nod of the head and directed them once again to the movement of Doctor Klinger's hands among the vestments. She could now already imagine the soft contours of the Round. Not quite spherical, not really oval, the perfection of roundness. She motioned to the students to make room behind Doctor Klinger's back. Then, with a deft draw of the left arm, the Doctor laid the loops of silk carefully upon the bed below the Round. His right hand moved quickly to a small pocket at the side of his gown and returned with a pair of scissors of carved gold, studded at the cross-piece with a large ruby. His long fingers seemed to fit naturally into the shaped handles. With a little "snip," he cut the ribbon, and the outer vestments fell away, leaving a thin, silvery gauze to cover the Round. The light from the window above the bed twinkled on the lattice of silver threads. Sighs and excited whispers rose from the students when they saw the forms of Doctor Klinger's masterpiece hiding behind the under-vestment.

Constance kept her eyes shielded by her arm. The final stage was near, and she so wanted John Peters to be with her. Something had to be wrong. As soon as he had heard that she was to take her Round, he had stopped calling her. Nor had he been seen at his usual haunts around the campus. Strange indeed. The Round was usually an occasion for rejoicing on the part of the boy or girlfriend, especially if the other had taken his or her Round, as she knew John Peters had.

Doctor Klinger straightened up, neatly placing the gold scissors back into his gown. He took pride in his artistic endurance., standing erect, elbows tucked into his side, hands clasped together in front of him, his scarlet gown billowing to the floor in long folds. He raised his eyes slowly to the roof where a candle burned softly below a small wooden cross entwined with the asp of medicine. The eyes of the students moved with him. The doctor stood head and shoulders above them as they crowded around. The Intern in her plain black gown motioned them back.

Dr. Klinger's lips moved imperceptibly within his jowled face. On a chronically ill or inoperative patient, such a face would have been ugly. But on the Doctor, it gave him a look of permanence. He was a rock of the past. The gray hair, still dark at the roots, grew down the sides of his cheeks like moss. His eyes were dark, always looking afar, hidden mysteriously beneath the lichen of his eyebrows. He exuded an air of timelessness, a dedicated will for the good. Constance peeped at him from under her arm. She felt secure.

A timid nurse in her grey gown edged her way through the white elbows of the students until she stood discretely at the Doctor's side. She held a silver tray upon which were two silver chalices. Dr. Klinger leaned across the bed, and gently guided his patient's arm from her face. How beautiful and innocent young girls in full bloom looked at this moment, he thought. The corners of his mouth flickered, her eyes bedazzled by his kindness. Then, gently kissing her cheek, he returned to his position.

With a delicate pinch of his forefinger and middle finger, he hitched up the loose sleeves of his gown and turned to the nurse who shook nervously. The Doctor gently squeezed her arm to calm her. A nervous honours student stepped forward holding out a pair of gold sequined gloves. Doctor Klinger held his arms out, palms upwards, elbows pointing to the ground, in the traditional manner of men of medicine. The student carefully slipped the gloves over the Doctor's long, slender fingers.

Now the time had come. Another nurse handed the Great Doctor a pair of golden scissors, this time a longer more slender pair, less ornately decorated, and he began to cut the small, embroidered loops which held the pleats of silver gauze over the Round. Soon it was loose, and the whole thing moved a little with each snip of the scissors. Finally, it was completely free, and it was only the shape of the Round which held the silver gauze in place.

"You must look down now, my dear," Doctor Klinger said warmly. "Oh! I can't! I can't!"

Doctor Klinger had already removed the silver gauze. The students crowded around to see. The Intern made a half-hearted attempt to hold them back. But she, too, was excited. And when they saw the work, their eyes opened wide, and they exuberantly chattered among themselves. Some of the younger girls could contain themselves no longer. They cried out, and ran to Constance, kissing her joyously. Constance was overcome and began to sob tears of joy. She had not yet looked down, but she knew that something very wonderful had happened.

Doctor Klinger quietly retreated into the background, and the nurse removed his gloves. He paused to watch the students, then, nodding to the nurse approvingly, he walked down the aisle between the cubicles, at first slowly, but gradually more and more quickly. His mind had already turned to the other important event of the day: the chief prosecutor had called an extraordinary meeting of the Colony Cabinet.

*

A slight buzz broke the silence as one of the hundred lights in the chandelier flickered and eventually faded out. Everyone looked towards Madam Fantasmag who managed in return to look at no one. A faint jingle sounded as the decorations hanging from her attendant's shoulder brushed against her bunched gray hair. She did not speak. Her face remained slightly amused, mostly expressionless. By a subtle sign, or perhaps by prearrangement, Chief Prosecutor Bart Iceland (pronounced "eye-land") opened the Cabinet meeting. He began in his gruff, half whispering voice.

"Great Gentlemen and Ministers. I am honoured to open this Extraordinary Meeting of the Cabinet, on behalf of our Esteemed Madam President Fantasmag."

"Obliged!" The Ministers chorused in unison.

"Now," the Chief Prosecutor extended the "ow" as though he was a priest saying 'Je-ho-vah,' "we pray that our personal prejudices and wants will be put aside, so that we may devote ourselves wholly and solely to the cause of the Madam and our Colony, so that real justice will be done."

"Our pledge!" Half sang like 'Amen.'

Then business. Everyone waited with baited breath. Chief Prosecutor Iceland beckoned to an attendant who came forward with a bundle of papers and passed out one to each member. Each Cabinet minister, in turn, tried to hide his eagerness to gobble up a copy, except Klinger who sat back quietly and waited until one had been neatly placed before him.

The Chief Prosecutor, behaving like a school teacher waiting for her students to finish reading a passage before testing their comprehension, had his attendant wheel him around the table. He made occasional comments, stopped here and there to peer over someone's shoulder.

"For the sake of convenience, we shall call this "Exhibit A." He paused, turned a page of the paper himself, and appeared to study it. "Please consider it carefully." He never gave any inkling of what was to follow, or why he had given it the status of an "exhibit."

EXHIBIT A read as follows:

Our Founding Fathers were moved by a deep devotion to the welfare of each other, a love of man, a tremendous faith in themselves as people—real people, It is in the spirit of their ideals, their great intentions, that I present this treatise. If I am at times critical of our Colony, it is only because I revere the great traditions established by our ancestors.

At the time of the settlement of our Colony, the pioneers were still forging their ideals into the actual functioning parts of a new society. Thus, they were forced, it was essential in fact, to attend only to the central and most general problems of the day, putting the peripheral issues in abeyance.

What were the pressing concerns of our Founding Fathers? They wanted to search out and obtain for everyone the richest, most fulfilling life; they wanted to raise to the highest level respect for the individual's right to partake of this richness, but at the same time never to force him to do so. It was the person's right to conduct his own life, provided it did not interfere with others. It was the individual's right to make agreements with others, and this right could never be interfered with by government. Out of this respect for the individual's sovereignty grew the unique system of private professions which flourished in the Colony until the Quiet Revolution. If advice or help were needed by anyone, he would go to his friends. Services of assistance were private arrangements.

The main weakness in our forefathers' charter was their narrow understanding of individual rights. They had not counted upon the possibility that often friends may be harsher judges of each other than are acquaintances, let alone government officials. They had not counted on the fact that people who have to be helped may resent it. Mutual helping began to disintegrate. The professions of medicine and law gradually became private monopolies, and pockets of people in need slowly discovered that they were living under the tyranny of professionalized fiefdoms. It soon became apparent that the precious life was enjoyed only by the professionals who fed off the lives of their patients.

Fortunately, before this problem crystallized enough to impel our grandfathers towards a violent and bloody revolution of the kind that has occurred in the history of other peoples, Madam Fantasmag brought about the quiet revolution, and the Great Practitioner Klinger provided the philosophical underpinning of the new deal. With the nationalization of the private professions, they aimed to completely eliminate inequality, and this they would achieve through universal Rounding.

Madam Fantasmag had been a well Rounded person herself, having begun her training very early in childhood. Some of the more liberal or progressive private professionals had introduced Rounding into their fiefdoms. Thus, it was no surprise and readily accepted by the people, when Madam Fantasmag and Doctor Klinger began to encourage all people to be Rounded. Klinger's classic book, *The Doctor and Your Self,* was published around that time, and local advisory treatment centres were set up throughout the Colony. "A well Rounded person is a healthy person" was the maxim.

There is no doubt that the Colony has benefited tremendously because of the work of these great leaders. Only one requirement now is ever made by the government upon its individual subjects: that they must be Rounded. The leaders pledged themselves to remove from the books as many laws as possible, along with their sanctions. The only strict requirement of any of us today is to be Rounded, healthy persons. Otherwise, we are free to live our own lives. Such freedom from oppression our forefathers could never have imagined!

There is no need to review the significant advances made in the theory and practice of Rounding. More people are clearly better Rounded today, and because of this, there is no doubt that life has become wonderfully enriched. The rich relationship that the doctor establishes with his patient, the experience of Rounding commonly shared with others—yet not shackling one to others as used to be the way—all of these contribute to a great feeling of community.

Community, it has been found, comes from a commonality of experience with other individuals but without obligation to them; and from a healthy devotional relationship between doctor and patient. By the exalting experience of the Round, life is enriched because of the new challenges one is forced to meet. The Rounded person discovers things about himself he never knew before.

The Quiet Revolution had its roots in the ideals of richness and community: the backbone of the old society. This is why it was not successful; it could not be a real revolution if it failed to reassess the priorities of the old society. The dangerous result was that by requiring everybody to be healthy, it assumed everybody to be sick, and did not recognize that some may be far sicker than others. Furthermore, I argue that universal Rounding, although it equalizes everyone to some extent, is not the only yardstick of health. Why can't there be unRounded persons who are healthy? This is the fundamental question to which I can only find one answer: people must undergo the same operation because Madam Fantasmag says so. I know many individuals who are indeed unRounded. I say that many of them are actually healthy. But given that they are not, why does the Colony blatantly ignore them? Why doesn't it make greater attempts to make them healthy? Why has there been no Commission to find out how many unRounded people there are? Why is there so little university research? I suspect that the reason is that it would hurt to acknowledge the answers: these people are impoverished and destitute, without the wherewithal to become Rounded. They represent, in fact, the dark passages in our history.

I know that some argue that because only very few demands are made of people, those who are not Rounded must accept the consequences. They are, in fact, according to the law, criminals. I understand that. But surely, it is unreasonable to expect everybody to be healthy.

"So what's so bad about this, Chief Prosecutor?" asked Doctor Klinger. The Chief Prosecutor merely answered by passing out another set of papers.

"These are the Clinician's reports," he announced, "one is of John Peters, the author of this subversive document, and the other is a person called Gilbert Manich. They have been good friends for about a year."

"And the charge?"

"There isn't any. This is only a preliminary inquiry."

"Why us, and not a medical court, then?"

"Honourable member, national security is involved. I suggest you read the Clinician's reports, then I will tell you the circumstances of the case. It is best that you read the reports before you know what the allegations are, so your minds will not be biased by their deeds. I think that is just."

"Yes, of course. Very fair indeed."

The ministers' hands stretched forward for the documents.

The Chief Prosecutor continued with the play: "For the sake of convenience we will label the report of John Peters, 'Exhibit B,' and that of Gilbert Manich 'Exhibit C.'"

EXHIBIT B

Gothic Hospital Diagnostic Clinic

CLINIC REPORT OF PATIENT 72 (John Peters)

General Impressions:

Patient 72 presents as a good looking, confident male, a little uneasy on first meeting, but gradually settles in. He has dark straight hair, stands erect, walks with a perfect gait, which suggests refined Rounding.

Attitude to the Clinical Period:

Shows an intense curiosity in the test situation. However, provided the examiner answers with firmness when asked inappropriate questions, patient's latent hostility is checked.

Test Results:

Body Symmetry. Patient obtained an overall B.S.Q. of 112, which is within the band of slightly above normal range.

Muscle Tone Profile. No apparent deviations of muscle tone were noted. Some light vibrations were found in the right upper arm, also the right leg above the Round. But the deviations are too slight to be significant and are probably due to fatigue. The general overall picture is within the normal range.

Total X-ray. No abnormalities found. Very faint opacity below the Round, but it is most likely of the type that is produced by the particular synthetic Round covers popularly worn these days.

Diagnosis:

Patient is normal, with possible latent hostile tendencies, which should be checked out. Clinical intuition suggests that this is probably related to Rounding adjustment.

EXHIBIT C

Gothic Hospital Diagnostic Clinic

CLINIC REPORT OF PATIENT 73 (Gilbert Manich)

General Impressions:

Patient impresses as an undersized male, skinny, slightly protruding hips. Walks with an affected, exaggerated gait, suggesting immature Rounding adjustment.

Attitude to the Clinical Period:

Patient displayed bravado and open hostility. This increased to such a level, that the examination had to be discontinued, and was conducted later with custodial supervision. Manich indulged in childish antics (e.g., standing on his hands, masturbating, etc.) and constantly used obscene language. He had to be physically prevented from displaying his Round.

Test Results:

Body-Symmetry: Patient obtained an overall B.S.Q. of 90, which is a borderline-subnormal range.

Muscle Tone Profile: Clear deviations above the Rounding area. Deviation pattern suggests that this patient is either unRounded or at least poorly adapted to the Round. His lack of cooperation, however, could also have contributed to the abnormal muscle tone patterning.

Total X-ray: No opacity or abnormality observed. However, this examiner is aware that Round covers can be purchased which will eliminate opacity. It is possible that this patient wears such a cover.

Diagnosis:

This patient may be an asymmetrical Roundopath. His constant regressions to childhood, mixed with erectile hyperactivity, suggest that he is fixated at the pre-Rounding stage. Deviations in muscle tone profile and possible opacity in total X-ray indicate that patient suffered severe trauma at Rounding. Further study, however, would be necessary to verify this hypothesis. Most important is the sub-normal B.S.Q. combined with asymmetrical hypersexual behaviour. This means that patient is constantly on the brink of losing control and is, therefore, a dangerous person.

*

"All right," announced the Chief Prosecutor, "here are the facts of the case. For the sake of those of you who are not lawyers, I'll just do a general summary, and won't detail the specific criminal charges. The two patients are accused of conspiracy to destroy the foundation of our society, the Round. They have established an extensive secret organization to provide people who are unRounded the means whereby they may keep their secret and cover it up. My investigators estimate that probably 5% of our adult population is unRounded, but, thanks to Manich's underground organization, they have been able to masquerade as Rounded. We have evidence that this organization is proliferating, and the number of unRounded seems to be increasing every day. The presence of such a large number of people who reject the basic binding value of our society is clearly a significant threat to our national security. Therefore, we decided to move now before it was too late. We have not had any social trouble in our Colony since the Quiet Revolution, and we don't want any. Our healthy and productive lives need not be spoiled by a disloyal few. The running of this secret organization we attribute to Gilbert Manich. The philosophical basis of the incipient terrorist group we attribute to John Peters. That is why I had my investigators obtain a copy of his term paper. It is clearly the precursor to seditious activity, although it may not be obvious to you at the moment. But I am convinced of it. The fact is the document represents the ideas underlying their next step, which is towards having themselves thought of as the product of a faulty society, rather than as the enemy of society. They hope, in short, to make their criminal, seditious conspiracy, respectable. Fortunately, I was on to their game very early, so we should be able to completely eliminate this disgusting underground enemy. With John Peters quietened, those we do not get will be unable to do anything alone, because as we all know, unRounded people are not very bright. In short, I think we have the problem well under control. However, the Madam did not want to deal with this secretly, because if anything leaked out, there would be a charge that the Madam was indulging in dictatorial government, which, of course, is not her want. She, therefore, after having thoroughly gone over all the details of the case, requested me to hold this extraordinary meeting to obtain your judgment. Shortly, we will bring in the suspects, and you may examine them. As Chief Prosecutor, I think that to let either of them free would seriously threaten public safety and health. But, of course, the final decision is up to you. Now, are there any questions?"

"What actual evidence do you have that this secret organization exists and is doing what you say?" asked Klinger.

"We have located an advanced factory. You may have noted the Clinician's reference to special Round covers. Well, he was partly on the track. When I bring the suspects in, you'll get a first-hand look at what they have been up to. The factory and its product are enough to convict them."

"And their direct relationship to the factory?"

"We have followed them for about a year now. We know they go into this facility often, but our agents have never been able to get inside the organization. It seems that unRounded people can pick those who are not unRounded simply by looking at them. So, without unRounded investigators, we haven't a chance. We don't want to raid the plant, to avoid creating panic."

"Let's see them."

"Bring them in!"

First Peters, then Manich were wheeled up to the space kept for them at the table. Bewildered and dumbfounded, they faced the six most powerful figures in the Colony. Manich immediately felt a bitter taste and spat loudly and messily out on the floor beside his chair. No one showed any recognition of the crude action. Peters wriggled in his seat, perspiration trickled down his back. He feared he was losing control of his eyes, which kept trying to turn upwards behind the lids. He clasped his hands together. It was Klinger who broke the silence and the threatening stares of curiosity.

"Mister Peters," Klinger addressed him in his deep voice, adding a touch of softness.

"Sir?"

"I was very interested to read your propaganda, which we all have before us. I think it makes some excellent points."

"Thank you, Sir," Peters smiled coyly. The Madam's eyes quickly flashed from Peters to Klinger and back.

Klinger continued, "Tell me, son, at what age were you Rounded?"

"Eighteen, Sir."

"And who performed the Round, my boy?"

"Doctor Ferstenteller. He's dead now I think," Peters added a little hastily.

"Oh, yes. He was an excellent practitioner. Tell me, have you met any of these poor unRounded people whose case you have taken it upon yourself to plead?"

The question was well phrased and placed Peters on the defensive. Indeed, what gave him the right to campaign on behalf of a minority of which he was not a part?

"Well, I don't know exactly, Sir. It's just that the ones I've met, by accident that is, though I tried to meet some as part of my research, well they seemed in such dire straits. It seems wrong to me to treat people who are different as unequal. I just felt I had to help them."

"Yes, but unRounded people are not just different, are they? They are severely disturbed, they're abnormal, perhaps subnormal, don't you think? Which is more than just being different. It inevitably means that they can't expect to receive the same rights as normal people."

"But why not?" Peters' eyes flashed, preparing for the verbal battle he had been expecting to fight for a long time.

"Well, a blind person shouldn't have the right to drive a car, should he?"

John Peters had no answer.

Klinger continued, "I was interested to read your explanation of why the Colony has ignored its unRounded people. I think I agree with your thesis there. But still, it does not logically follow that the people should, therefore, be sought out and helped, does it?"

"But if you recognize the existence of a minority which has been discriminated against, how can you say that?"

"Certainly I acknowledge that such people exist, but only abstractly. That is enough for me, for if I meet an unRounded person, I should see to it that he becomes Rounded because my philosophy convinces me that this is the better, richer, more challenging way of life. Therefore, it is best that I do not recognize the actual or real existence of the minority group, or I should be forced to impose upon them my philosophy. And as everyone knows, I have never supported that. I have never performed a Round on anyone against his will. Most people are happy to have it done. It would defeat the whole purpose to force it upon them."

"Yes, I agree with that. I certainly would oppose such tyranny. But do you not think that you have made the assumption that those who are not Rounded are so because they don't want to be? It is my thesis, on the contrary, that the majority of them do want to be Rounded, but they are denied the opportunity."

Peters felt inspired. He found the Great Doctor fascinating to listen to. He seemed to understand very clearly what he was trying to say.

"Yes, to some extent you are right," nodded the Great Doctor. "I have made that assumption. But my point is still partly valid. By establishing research in that area, by identifying this group in practice, you will, in a sense, be hunting them down, if you will excuse the use of such colourful words."

Peters was speechless. Was it possible that Klinger shared the views of Manich? Had the Professor plucked out the radical eye of his thesis?

"Mister Peters, you realize that our concern about your propaganda is guided solely by our concern for the welfare of the people. We were worried, or should I say, the Chief Prosecutor was concerned—he very sensibly brought you to our notice— that should your ideas be disseminated amongst the people, we may be confronted with serious social unrest. Which would mean innocent people would get hurt. So, although you may have had good intentions, it was necessary for us to look into the matter. You understand?"

"Yes, sir. Although now, I'm not sure that my ideas were all that radical."

"Radical? They're the basis for revolution! That's what they are, Mister Peters!" thundered the Chief Prosecutor.

"Well, I used to think so," Peters replied trying to be cooperative, "but now, after Professor Klinger's comments, I don't know."

"You don't know?" The Chief Prosecutor turned to him abruptly, almost sneering. "You don't know? You are playing with dynamite. You recognize that people who are the dark side of our society, those completely different to ourselves, entirely contrary to us, should be treated equally, as though they were the same as us! You are destroying the whole moral basis of our society! How will you tell the difference between right and wrong? What is the purpose of going through the challenge of Rounding, the self-sacrifice, only to find that those who do not do it, receive the same benefits as yourself? Where is the justice in that, Mister Peters?"

"Well, I—"

"The fact is, Mister Peters, you are playing with ideas that are too big for you! You have deceived yourself, and worse, you are trying to deceive us!"

The sweat poured down Peters' back, and he began to quiver like a fish. The Madam looked at him with her open, pale eyes. The other ministers stared and frowned, not quite understanding the Prosecutor's barrage of words.

"Sir, I never have—"

But at this point, Manich rose bodily out of the wheelchair, and, penis in hand, directed a stream of urine upon the polished table. The stream splashed out in all directions and droplets rebounded and spattered over the papers before the ministers. Brutus, the Madam's attendant, ever mindful of the President's safety, pulled back her chair, and lunged in full flight across the top of the table. only to be fired upon by Manich's deadly aim. His legs off the floor, and having only one arm, Brutus was stuck on his belly, thrashing around like a turtle out of water. Attendants quickly pulled other ministers out of range. Peters wanted to urge Manich to stop but resisted. The Chief Prosecutor, eyes ablaze, lifted the telephone and rattled off a chain of commands. Before Manich could empty his bladder, a Custodian appeared at the door, casually dragging his stethoscope behind him.

"You bunch of bloated pigs!" Manich yelled. "Why don't you murder us to be done with it? Why don't you be honest for a change?"

Attendants forced him back into his seat, and he sat there apoplectic. A Custodian came up behind and stretched out his huge arms, wrapping them round Manich's chest in a bear hug. By sticking out his gut into Manich's back, he was able to bend him back so far his spine could have snapped. No one moved.

"Really, Madam, please stop this brutal behaviour before us. It's demeaning," said Klinger, who had devoted his life in the Colony to the eradication of violence.

Manich gasped for breath, still managing to kick his legs up against the table, scratching it badly, almost turning it over. The Madam looked at her Chief Prosecutor, who immediately ordered more attendants to hold Manich's arms and legs until he was strapped into his chair.

"I demand severe punishment for this—this criminal, this traitor, this psychopathic killer!" raved one of the ministers.

The smallest, weasel-looking Cabinet member stirred and spoke. He was Dr. Foote, the newest member of the Cabinet, and the youngest.

"Punishment," wheezed Dr. Foote, "is not necessary for either of them. If you had been able to understand the Clinician's reports you would realize that step-wise Rounding can be profitably applied to these patients. Furthermore, my experience tells me," he paused for effect, "that this patient Manich is unRounded!"

The Chief Prosecutor appeared unperturbed by this revelation. but Klinger and the other Cabinet members shifted in their seats. It had never occurred to them that there could be someone in this very room, one of them, someone unRounded. With the exception of Klinger, they had never seen an unRounded person in their lives. Dr. Foote sat bolt upright, thoroughly impressed by his own revelation.

The Chief Prosecutor replied coolly, "I'm only a lawyer, I'm afraid, and I can't really accept that hypothesis simply upon the basis of a few tests whose validity is questionable anyway."

"All right," replied Foote cockily, "let's look and see."

"But that would be obscene!" complained one member.

"Undress him!" grumbled another.

The Chief Prosecutor quickly eyed the cabinet ministers. Looking at someone's Round was an immoral act. It was never done, except at the moment of "birth" when the Round was unwound by the likes of Dr. Klinger. He flashed a sideways glance at the Madam, who gave no indication of her position.

"We'll take a vote," he decided. "Of course we have the right as Cabinet ministers to view the Round, working for the good of the Colony. But I think it should be a unanimous decision. Those in favour of looking at Manich's Round, say, 'Aye.'"

There was some hesitation as each one waited for the other to vote, but they all fell into line when Klinger showed his affirmation.

"Then we all agree. Take off his clothes, everything. We need only the Custodian and two attendants. The rest of you leave us, but be on call. And Brutus, you stand at the ready, if it's okay with you, Madam Fantasmag."

The big man struggled back to his feet without anyone's assistance The Madam shook her head and narrowed her eyes a little at her Prosecutor. She never allowed anyone to deal with Brutus and was displeased. The Prosecutor, carried away by the moment, had forgotten himself.

The attendants removed all Manich's clothes, beginning from the top and working down. Why it had to be all the clothes, Manich never knew. The whiteness of his body glowed under the brightness of the chandelier. There was an air of excitement and apprehension as though a strip-tease were in progress. Manich's chair was wheeled back a little from the table so that all ministers could see everything to the floor. Now he displayed no resistance; now there was nothing left on him but the Round cover. The attendants looked up to the Prosecutor for guidance. They couldn't bring themselves to actually do it.

"Doctor Foote," Chief Prosecutor Iceland asked in a congenial tone, gesturing towards Manich, "it is a doctor's job, after all." He smiled.

Foote was flattered. "Of course," he said, and an attendant wheeled him forward. Foote leaned downwards and stretched towards the end of Manich's leg. He began to unbuckle the leather straps around the leg, his fingernails clicking quietly against the shiny aluminium, the buckles occasionally clinking like sleigh-bells It looked like a genuine D-leg, which meant that there should be a Round under it. He touched it here and there with his fingers, knocked on it with his knuckles. There was no typical hollow sound as there usually was with a D-leg. He felt just below the knee, the joint seemed to be normal. Foote gulped and sat back into his chair. The blood had gone to his head while he was leaning downwards, and he waited for it to clear.

"Gentlemen," his voice quavered a little, "I think I was wrong. From my external examination, this patient is Rounded."

But the Chief Prosecutor was not prepared to let it go. He scowled: "You started it! Now finish it!"

Foote was so upset at having been wrong, he found himself obeying, and immediately leaned down to continue the unwrapping. All the buckles were undone, and he pressed the catch behind the leg. With a hollow click, the leg came off, leaving exposed the Rounded part below the knee, covered in the traditional silver gauze. He caught the ribbon that was tied around the gauze to keep it in place, and with a quick movement of the fingers, as though he were using a polishing cloth, he snatched it off and sat up straight.

All the Cabinet ministers gaped. Peters closed his eyes. The Madam appeared disinterested. The Chief Prosecutor smiled smugly, which Klinger noticed, realizing that the Prosecutor had not yet played his trump card. Manich, seemingly in a stupor slowly awoke, his hands automatically groping their way to his Rounded leg, to feel the calloused skin. He moaned, shaking his head from side to side, crying, "No! No! No!" The Ministers continued to stare.

Peters' eyes remained firmly closed, his teeth clenched together. He knew what was coming. The Chief Prosecutor gave the order.

"Disrobe the next patient."

Peters shook with tension and fear and summoned all his strength and training to prevent losing his head. He closed his eyes, but only saw images of a guillotine blade falling down upon him from way up high. He bit his tongue hard to keep himself in check. His time had come.

Doctor Foote came forward to undo the leg. This time, he made no attempt to examine and diagnose first, he just went straight ahead and undid the leather straps, then slid his fingers around the smooth aluminium to find the catch. It gave the same tiny clicking noise, but this time, instead of the leg coming away as expected, it opened up all the way down the front, and under it could be seen the shiny white skin of Peters' leg, running from the knee all the way down to the ankle. Foote gulped, and stared, as though he had just uncovered a golden nugget.

The Chief Prosecutor without even looking announced, "Yes, gentlemen. This is the great deceiver of us all. He is unRounded!"

Foote tugged at the apparatus, then Peters leaned down, and pressed another hidden catch. The whole leg cover came off, leaving in its place an impressive right foot, the toes wiggling to relieve cramp, the skin pale from lack of light.

"This is disgraceful!" exclaimed one of the members.

"This, gentlemen, is what I wanted you to see," announced the Prosecutor, as he picked up the aluminium apparatus which Foote had let drop to the floor. "This, gentlemen, is a D-D-Leg, the term for a dummy-dummy-leg, and these are what are made in Manich's factories. They can be worn by unRounded people who, provided they practice their gait, can pass for being Rounded. I submit to you that this man, John Peters, is far more dangerous than Manich because he is a deceiver.

Peters looked up, shaking a little, his face pale, his lips a dark red. He looked beseechingly to Klinger.

"Professor Klinger, I had hoped you would understand. It was a mistake."

"Ummm, I'm not sure what you're asking, Mr. Peters."

"He's begging for mercy!" someone scoffed. "And I say we don't give him any. Off with his leg!"

"Stop it!" the Prosecutor growled, "we've had enough of those words today! Now, Mr. Peters, what have you to say for yourself?"

"All I want to say is although now that I have been uncovered, I look different to you, I am not really all that different—"

"But you're unRounded!"

"Yes, but with my cover, and my practice, you would never know. I mean, before you knew about this, you treated me as a Rounded person, and I behaved as a Rounded person. It was only my association with my friend Manich that gave me away."

"But that was before we knew. Now we do, and so now you're different."

"But if I put the cover back on, walk with the proper gait, as far as outward appearances are concerned, I'm the same as you."

"But we will still know that behind your act, is the real you, which is unRounded. We will still know that you are different."

"But by the way I behave in society, I'm no different. And if you have to continue suspecting that behind my act I am really un-Rounded, you'll have to do it with everyone. Otherwise, you will never know who is real and who is not."

Peters had gone over this speech many times before and always enjoyed it. The argument had an unbeatable quality. It always seemed to him so unrebuttable, that he doubted its logic. Yet he could not find any flaws in it.

The Chief Prosecutor, obviously annoyed, broke in. "Incorrect on two counts. First, we know about you. That changes everything. Shows of compliance are not enough. Devotion is required. It is irresponsible, indeed, traitorous, to say or do one thing, but believe or do the opposite in secret. It is, in fact, a conspiracy against the State. Second, you imagine we would not go as far as suspecting everyone. Wrong again. Depending on the outcome of future investigations, we may examine everyone in the Colony, and find out just who have treasonous illnesses and who don't."

Klinger sat up abruptly.

"Chief Prosecutor, I do not like that kind of talk," he complained. "I will take no part in a decision that leads to the complete sur-veillance of the people. We are here to preserve their freedom. The philosophy of the Colony does not require that they give up their souls to the State!"

"So you agree with this traitor? Outward compliance is sufficient, even though we know that secretly, he does not comply?"

"But you made the point yourself, Honourable Prosecutor. The fact that we know about him changes things. He no longer secretly does not comply. All of his behaviour is now overt, as far as I can see. In fact, if all of his behaviour is aimed towards compliance, such as his extensive training in the proper gait, and so on, then surely the fact that he is unRounded is not as serious. I mean, it's his actual behaviour that counts, not what he is."

Klinger was amazed at what he had said and would have liked to take it back.

"He is an enemy," another member spluttered, "that's what he is. So if we value ourselves, we cannot value him. He must be eliminated."

The crispness of the statement surprised them all and gladdened the heart of the Chief Prosecutor. "I could have not said it better," he smiled.

"But that's unjust," Foote now joined in. "Surely his history makes it clear that it is not his fault that he is unRounded, and that he has done everything in his power to at least join us. Surely, that is in his favour?"

"The issue is much bigger than this individual, Dr. Foote," replied the Chief Prosecutor. "That's the trouble with you doctors. You never look past the individual to the society that has to put up with him. What you say about this individual may be right. Perhaps he is not responsible, and maybe he has tried. But that's not the point. It's what he represents that is serious. He poses a threat to the very basis of our existence. If we tolerate him, we destroy ourselves. Frankly, I'd rather it the other way around."

"But aren't there any in-betweens?" pleaded Peters. "You think in black and white terms. Surely, because I am able to walk like you, even though I am really not the same as you, makes me different from a person who is not like you, and doesn't try to walk like you?"

"When it comes to defending the very basis of one's existence, there are no in-betweens," replied the Prosecutor coldly.

"Then what about the people I treat?" Foote asked. "Surely, we have moved on from that old fashioned view? We no longer punish people, and punishment is surely applied to one's enemies. But treatment, and our widespread use of it, recognizes that a different person is not all bad?"

The Prosecutor dealt a swift response. "Your treatment is simply another word for punishment. I would have thought that were obvious to us all."

Foote was outraged, professionally insulted. He had chosen to be a doctor so he could help unfortunate and unhealthy people. Helping them was his overriding concern. He always became frustrated and annoyed at these meetings of the Cabinet, because the ministers did not seem especially aware of helping the unfortunate. He had a right to be impatient, in his opinion. And now, this brazen, thick-headed lawyer, had the audacity to classify his treatment methods as punishment.

"Honourable Prosecutor, I insist on an apology. That's the most insulting, outrageous remark ever addressed to me."

"I'll have it stricken from the record," the Prosecutor smiled sardonically.

Klinger spoke again. "I want to make a suggestion. It is my recommendation that Mr. Peters be set free. Not only that, but I would like to suggest that he be given an official position in the Colony to work with unRounded people. They must require lots of training to acquire the proper gait, and I gather that Mr. Peters is an expert. Is this what you have been doing at Manich's factories?"

"Yes, sir. I train people in their gait, and use of the D-D-Leg."

The doctor continued. "As far as I can see, as benevolent governors of the Colony, we cannot refuse his plea to help these unfortunate people. We could, perhaps, appoint a committee to go into the matter further. Maybe a return to informal treatment may be worth trying. I must say again, I do not want to force anyone to take the Round. I don't expect that everyone will want to take it or be able to take it, so if someone with good will wants to help them, I think that's fine. Surely our society is strong enough to withstand a little tolerance."

"Yes, I think that is an excellent suggestion," agreed another Cabinet member, but then Foote spoke up.

"I believe this is going beyond what is needed. It's one thing to allow Peters some freedom, but another to actually give him an official position. After all, he is a sick person. By giving him such a position, we condone the sickness, which is entirely contradictory to the very basis of our health system. I cannot understand how the great doctor can suggest such a thing since his whole theory of Rounding is based upon putting considerations of society before the individual. I've criticized his position on that issue many times before, on the grounds that he sees Rounding as an individual's contribution to society, rather than an intrinsically rewarding and enriching experience itself, one that unlocks the individual from his predetermined physical existence. Society will always remain imperfect. Our answer is to help the individual to adapt. Mr. Peters' "adaptation" seems to me to place greater demands upon the people. It makes them, first, decide to go through life deceiving others, and second, requires of them a long and rigorous training schedule. Surely it is less of a demand to take a Round. I say, therefore, that we should insist in this case that Mr. Peters be Rounded, preferably by my modern method which places emphasis on the conscious experience of Rounding, rather than

Klinger's old fashioned method of anaesthetics. My recommendation, therefore, is that Peters be sent to my clinic along with Manich, and undergo the Round. Furthermore, if this Round is successful, which I think it will be, I suggest that our welfare agencies be completely overhauled and that the Colony agree to administer Rounds to anyone completely free of charge.

"A thoroughly excellent recommendation," applauded another member.

The Chief Prosecutor, however, did not respond as Foote expected him to. Instead, he looked to Klinger.

"Foote has, of course, always been confused about the role of the Round," said Klinger. "He is unable to see beyond the four walls of a clinic. If you remember your history, you know that there was a period just before the Quiet Revolution, when private doctors set themselves up as lords over their patients and controlled every aspect of their lives. Had it not been for the Madam's intervention, there would have been a bloody and violent revolution. As it was, she established the medical profession as the basis of society, and, happily, redirected its activities. But I now see that the doctor is always potentially the tyrant, because we have not yet discovered either complete cures or even what range of sicknesses exists. I know that the remedy proposed by Dr. Foote sounds inviting, but to do it would be like applying ointment only on one pimple in a whole rash. We must discover the cause of the illness. And I see now that we will never do that by treating it."

The Prosecutor lost patience. "Professor Klinger. We can look for causes another time. The tradition of the Colony is that a crime must be treated—or a sickness must be punished—whichever formula suits you. And that is that. The feeling of the Cabinet is against you. Sorry—"

"I'll not—" Klinger began, but was interrupted by another member.

"No, it's not. I supported his plan from the beginning, and I still do. It's the most sensible and cautious. As the social scientist in this group, I understand Professor Klinger's concern totally. Perfectly reasonable."

The Prosecutor's ear lobes went red when he realized his mistake. It could have cost him the decision, for although the vote would be three-two against Klinger, he could see that Klinger intended to fight.

"I'll not give in on this," Klinger persisted. "I've had time to think, and I'm sure I'm right. Enforced Rounding is not the answer to this patient under these circumstances."

"Klinger, you'll have to go along with the vote. Who is in favour of Klinger's—"

Before he could finish, Klinger cut in again and addressed Madam Fantasmag. It was a gamble. He had watched her eyes flash to Peters on occasions, and he knew the way she thought. Unless she was planning to completely discard him for the Prosecutor, she would agree, or at least almost agree with him. "Madam Fantasmag, are you going to let this happen?" he asked.

All eyes moved to the grand old lady. Her pale eyes stared out at them all as though from a portrait. The wrinkles on her face contorted as she moved her jaw in a chewing action. Suddenly, an eruption occurred, and she smiled. Her words flopped out, and her voice rattled as though she were being jolted over a cobblestone road on a dray.

"My dear Klinger, you are so tenacious." She looked, however, not at Klinger, but at Peters. "I am impressed by this boy's performance in the face of we six old ogres. It was a great test, and he passed well, not like his friend, whose disposition you have so wisely decided. But this boy, I think, should be given a chance. However, my good Klinger, you cannot really expect us to make him an official. He is, after all, a criminal."

The Madam cackled a crackling sort of laugh. "Peters may be set free for a period of six months, after which we will reconsider his position. If my Chief Prosecutor decides things are not going well, he may call another meeting. After the six months, we will also reconsider what to do with unRounded people. In the meantime, Peters must have nothing at all to do with the unRounded. At first sign of this, he will be detained. However, he is such a particularly interesting case, I want him to report to me once a week. He must also report to Klinger each week for discussions. I'll leave it to the two of you to arrange that. Mr. Peters' first visit with me will be tomorrow morning." She turned as far as she could to Brutus and smiled. "Meanwhile, he may as well stay the night. See that he is made comfortable, for he will be a palace guest."

*

Cloud hung low, and the air of the night embraced her. It was warm, and the rich aroma of the exhaling chestnut leaves filled her nostrils. Her feet landed with a plop on the carpet of old leaves that puffed and panted as the rubber tips of her crutches made their dent. The cloud diffused the light of the moon into a kind of fluorescence. It seemed like a friendly night to Constance; a night when the sounds and shadows spoke to her. She felt as though she were on show, and tried to hold her head up high allowing her ebony hair to wave gently from shoulder to shoulder. Unused to the crutches, she stopped for a moment to catch her breath. Her eyes felt moist, and she stared upwards as though trying to find the secret source of the night light. The sounds of the chestnut grove were magnified. Insects were chirping, rasping, clicking. She listened for the sound of her lover, thought she heard a faint, metallic clicking sound. Why had John Peters insisted on this place? She would have preferred him to sneak through her bedroom window.

Constance breathed in deeply, and her heart gave a faint flutter. This was a lover's night. Her Round throbbed a little, but she pushed on, and the sounds of the evening were forced into the background by her steps. She stopped again and scratched her wrist. The aluminium of her crutches clanked a little as they came together. She had no watch, but she knew it was time. He was close to her.

"John?" she inquired meekly. The insects spoke up in chorus. There was a "plop" as a chestnut fell beside her.

"Over here!"

Constance looked to the voice. She was a little frightened and bit her lip. Her Round was hurting a little. She frowned and stared into the thick air.

"Come, darling!" John Peters emerged from the shadows, and before she knew what was happening, he had whisked her off her feet, leaving the crutches to drop stiffly to the ground. He carried her across to the edge of a hollow that ran down to the trunk of a large tree, and gently emptied her from his arms so that she went rolling down to the bottom. Old leaves, soft and a little damp, stuck to her as she rolled. Constance giggled.

"John?" she called in her thin, shaky voice.

"My little Round!" John leaned over her, looking into her dark, moist eyes. He stuck out his tongue and licked the tip of her nose. It tickled her, and her eyelashes fluttered. She could hardly contain her excitement. She wanted to talk as well, ask questions, but knew not to. John slowly closed down upon her. Taking deep, long breaths, he seemed super calm, as though he had practiced these movements many times over. His breath tickled the whiskers of his upper lip, then moistened Constance's cheek. He allowed his nose just to touch the outer corner of her eye, then moved softly across her face till their lips met. He paused. Constance almost gasped. Her mouth opened, lips red and full, then she lunged at him, flinging her arms around his square shoulders, pushing her mouth on his, fingering his lovely dark hair, pushing her thumb against the side of his solid neck. Blood pulsed through her veins, the pores of her skin opened themselves to the night air.

"John! So long! Take me! Take me!" she cried.

"Easy! Easy!" Peters gently slid his arms around her, and rolled over onto his back, taking her with him, bearing her full weight. She kissed him passionately all over, her eyes closed, oblivious to their surroundings. Peters carefully responded, his eyes fixed open, staring somewhere off into the darkness behind her. He frowned slightly. Although he too had dreamed of this occasion, he had also feared it as a revelation, always worried how she would respond when she discovered his secret. But now he realized that the problem was not with her, but himself. They rolled over again and came to rest on their sides. She caressed him, pushed herself close. He stroked her hair and twiddled her ear between his fingers. He convulsively swallowed a large mouthful of saliva. Constance lowered her hands and began the exciting fiddling with his buttons. His hand slid under her dress, catching the old leaves as it went, then accidentally, touching her Round cover. Reflexively, he withdrew his hand, as though he had touched a hot iron.

"Go ahead, darling," Constance sighed, "I don't mind, really. You know I believe in natural love. Otherwise, we wouldn't be here now."

Peters' mind wandered into the darkness. The palace and the cabinet members, and Manich darted before his eyes. Once again his fingers touched her covered Round, and Manich's episode before the Cabinet swept into view. Preoccupied with the vision, he allowed his chest to collapse a little under Constance's pressure and had to gasp for breath. She replied by more delicately fondling him with her slender hands. She removed all his clothes. A sudden breeze wafted across their little dale, rustling the leafy bushes, bending the hairs on his body. Peters returned to the present. He walked his fingers up Constance's back, unsnapped her bra, stroking her lightly and slowly.

"Take me with you, sweetheart," he heard himself whispering. Constance tore off the rest of her clothes. Her fingers dropped down to his Round. First the leather straps. Then she felt for the latch, and the little click sounded. But the D-leg did not come away, so Constance gave it a little tug. But instead of coming apart as she expected, the leg opened up straight down the shin, her little finger slipping in through the opening, to feel the smooth skin of his shin bone. She caught her breath.

"John, I...I...I'm not imagining things am I?"

"No."

"But why didn't you tell me?" Her eyes watered a little.

"I wanted to, but I couldn't do it."

"But I love you. I can understand—"

"I know, I know. It wasn't that I was afraid that I would lose you. Believe me. I didn't want to hurt you, that's all."

"Oh, John darling! You lovable fool! I wouldn't care if you had three legs. All the more to love!"

They rolled apart, and she looked at him. "But why aren't you, John?"

"Not now—."

"But John, I should—"

He placed a finger on her moist lips. She smiled and closed her eyes.

"Feel me," she purred. She took his hand gently in hers and carried it down to her Rounded leg. She pushed his hand against the silk cover. John let his hand hang limp. He closed his eyes, hoping that this would prevent Constance from seeing into him. The thought of touching a Round repulsed him. He winced and tried to pull his hand away.

"Don't be frightened! Here, darling, here! Feel! Isn't it beautiful? Didn't Doctor Klinger do a fantastic job?" Constance had removed the cover and pulled John's reticent hand down, and his fingers just touched the stump of her leg where it had been amputated below the knee. The contact made her jump. It was pure touch.

"Why, it's so smooth and, and, Round!" John exclaimed.

"Of course it's round, silly!!"

"But why doesn't the bone make a bump?"

"Doctor Klinger. He's an artist. It's so symmetrical, don't you think?" Constance sat up and was looking down at her shortened leg. She still had hold of his hand, tickling herself with his fingers. John was astonished. To feel, it was nowhere nearly as ugly as he had imagined. He kept his eyes closed.

"John! Look at it, sweetheart!"

He couldn't. Not at the stump of the girl he loved. "Plenty of time for looking," he whispered, and he rolled over her and pulled her down beneath him. Constance gave a little squeal. She fought her way out of his arms, and with her tongue drew a wet line from his neck right down to his toes. She kissed every toe, all ten of them, and played with each of them in turn. She hugged them to her face and chewed them mischievously. John dared to open his eyes, and saw to his horror the butt of her leg staring him in the face. It was a dark, inflamed red, and it reminded him of the behinds of monkeys he had seen at the zoo. He gulped, and stared up at the spreading chestnut tree, wishing it would fall down upon him. Lying still, he closed his eyes again, allowing Constance to play. He would have to leave it all to her.

At last, Constance returned from the outer limits of his toes, and with great effort, lurched upwards, and sat astride him, where she began to move rhythmically while he stroked her freely hanging breasts. The sheer force of her enthusiasm began to penetrate the constriction in John's brain. He allowed his hand to slip down from her breast on to her Round. She gave out a deep sigh, which served to urge him on. She leaned back a little and caressed him. John hugged her closely, and with a big lunge, rolled around and on top of her. The touch of her Round fired him now, and blood pumped furiously to the centres of their bodies. The air closed around them, and the old, brown leaves stuck to their backs as they rolled over and over as one.

The insects once again took up their song. Constance clutched Peters so closely, it told him that she must never know how her Rounded leg repulsed him. Had he told her that he was unRounded, would she have refused the Round herself? But that would have been impossible. They unlocked, and lay quietly on their backs side by side, holding hands. The insects and night noises seemed different now; each sound meant a pair of eyes. They put on their clothes and sat up against the tree, John holding her close to him. Constance dreamed happily of their future together. They slept in each other's arms almost until dawn when they went their separate ways, John insisting that they must not be seen together.

Constance realized, as she made her way home that she knew nothing of what had happened to him, she had been so full of the night, her first natural love. She had sensed his tension in the tautness of his body. What would her father say if he knew that she had made love to a criminal? She smiled. Or had even made love to anyone! She felt secure, even courageous as she approached the door of her home. If mother or father were waiting up for her, she would say she had been out, and it was none of their business.

She saw no one. Her father had paused at the front of the house, leaning his D-leg against one of the foot racks along the sidewalk. When he saw the light of Constance's bedroom go out, he quietly let himself into the house and made a phone call. It was the Chief Prosecutor calling. Soon, the faint rumble of a motor interrupted the silence of the dying night. As it became louder, Peters who had emerged from the trees into an empty street, knew that he should run off and hide somewhere. Instead, he sat on the gutter, his head clenched between his hands as the noise of the engine grew louder and louder. He recognized it to be the hospital van, and pressed his hands to his ears, hoping to drown out the noise. The ambulance screeched to a halt. The doors banged open and heavy hands gripped his armpits as the medical officers half lifted, half dragged him into the ambulance.

He expected the dungeons, but he was flabbergasted to find himself delivered by Brutus into the inner depths of the palace, and seated at a small marble topped table supported by gilt wrought iron legs. He faced Madam President Fantasmag. Dumbfounded, he simply gaped at her wrinkled, wizened face. Her fox's eyes twinkled.

"Orange juice?" her gravelled voice jumped across at him. Peters was unable to answer. She continued, "My boy! If you are to do well today, you must have a proper breakfast." Her head jerked a little, and a smile twitched the corners of her mouth.

"Oh, yes. Thank you."

"Brutus!"

"Madam President?"

"Bring orange juice!"

*

A week had gone by, and the day for Manich's first stepwise Rounding treatment had arrived. He had been subjected to many different tests, they had photographed both his unRounded leg and his Rounded leg from every possible angle, and Doctor Foote had conducted many conferences with his assistants in hushed, serious tones. White clad attendants limped in, smiling broadly and all speaking at once:

"This is the big day!" they chirped.

Manich closed his eyes and gritted his teeth. There was simply nothing he could do. He had tried one last time upon his arrival at Foote's sanatorium to upset them all by flying into a rage. Even knocked the teeth out of one of the assistants. Since then he had been strapped into the bed, even when he was immobilized by Foote's drugs which paralysed him but made him acutely aware of the extremities of his limbs. Another injection this morning had made his foot begin to throb, and now it was causing him excruciating pain. One of the attendants knocked the bed, and his foot felt as though it would burst. He could no longer keep his teeth clenched together, and shrieked so loudly that everyone stopped still. Doctor Foote approached him quietly.

"Don't worry, my boy, we'll have that pain off in no time. You'll see." Foote placed his hands on his hips in a businesslike fashion. "You're in for a great experience."

Manich gritted his teeth again, screwed his eyes shut, hoping to suppress the excruciating shooting pains. Foote looked across to his assistants.

"I think we had better begin the preliminary work," he said. "Bring me fifty mils of H-S-4 please nurse."

The injection was given, and Manich fell silent, his heaving chest making the only noise. The backs of his eyelids glowed bright red. The attendants untied the bed straps and carefully lifted him onto a trolley. His body was completely naked except for a small gauze cover over his Round. On the point of hysteria, Manich wanted to thrash his arms and legs around but was unable to move. He heard the reverberating bang as the trolley hit the double doors and was shunted forward into the operating room. Once again he felt strong hands under his body, and he was thrust upon the operating table. The jolt shook his eyes open, and to his horror, he saw what seemed like hundreds of faces staring down at him through the ceiling. He could smell the breath of every surgeon and every assistant. Sickly smells they were. Manich recognized Foote by his dark eyes. He was given another injection as they taped other tubes and gadgets to his body. The upper end of the operating table was raised slightly so that he was in a half-sitting, half-lying position. A silk screen was inserted above and to the end of his body, and he saw, to his horror, the complete and magnified image of his legs from the hips down. One of the attendants pressed a button, and the angle of the view changed. The legs could be viewed from any angle.

"As this is your first stepwise Round," Foote informed him, "you won't get to use this gadget, as you'll have your time cut out just coping with the experience. But by your fifth, you will savour every moment of it, I promise you!"

Manich closed his eyes and ran his tongue over his teeth. Foote adjusted the microphone around his neck and gave a short, chesty cough. The room fell silent.

"Ladies and gentlemen of the profession," Foote tilted his head backward and scanned the audience above, "I hope you have read the background materials of this patient. It is a challenging case. The week's preparations have been the following: We began by administering pain localization serum, starting with five mils and increasing at a rate of 12 each day for five days, when the patient reported severe pain in his foot. Ten minutes ago, we gave him fifty mils of H-S-4, and a booster as soon as he was placed on the operating table. Limb Immobilizer serum has been necessary continually because of the patient's extreme violence. If you turn to page three, you will see the treatment profile I have planned for him. This is the first of five Rounds. The present one will be applied to the left leg below the knee, the next two close to the thigh on each leg, then, depending upon progress, both arms at the elbow. There is, of course, always the possibility of modification should the patient improve more slowly or more rapidly than we expect. We could, for example, begin by Rounding at each finger joint, and gradually work up the elbows. But it's hard to make predictions about progress at this stage. Because my active awareness method has not been widely used as yet, we do not have enough data upon which to base predictions. Nurse, administer the second H-S-4 booster."

There was a dull rustling in the audience. Dr. Foote sensed an unease. He looked up and continued his commentary.

"Perhaps I should briefly outline the rationale behind my method. The great Professor Klinger, as we all know, pioneered the art of Rounding as a therapeutic experience. However, under Professor Klinger's procedure, the patient only experiences the Round after it is done, sometimes weeks after when it is finally unwrapped. He thus misses out on the essential, real experience of the separation of his parasitic limb from his being, which under my method he sees and feels immediately it occurs. This unique experience allows the patient to gain keen, intense insight into himself and when he sees his 'alter limb' separated from his body, he has the experience of seeing his 'alter limb' as others would see it. Although it no longer is a part of him physically, he psychologically knows it is a part of him. It, therefore, serves both to enhance his own individual identity as separate from the rest of the world, but at the same time brings home to him that he is also physically very much a part of that world. It is the intensity of the experience of separation that is important, for by seeing it all in a heightened psychological state, the separation becomes something extraordinary, something that will never be forgotten. An image to last forever. In short, we provide him with an indestructible identity. Now, are there any questions?"

"Yes," a distorted voice came through the loud speaker system connecting the gallery to the operating room, "does this mean, Doctor, that your method places no importance on Doctor Klinger's unwrapping ceremony?"

"Exactly!" Foote smiled, pleased with the question. "I consider that method to be old-fashioned, ritualistic witchery!"

"But isn't what you are doing just as ritualistic?"

"Certainly not! What you see here are procedures necessary for the accomplishment of real tasks, and real experiences. Klinger's rituals are rituals because they deal with artificial and unreal experiences. Mine are scientific procedures designed to achieve a particular objective. Klinger's are ritualistic in short run, and overall, religious in connotation."

The audience remained quiet. Foote continued, "let us begin shall we?"

The doctor looked down at Manich's leg, then across to his face. He stood back on his heels, smiling, holding his hands and arms upward as though holding an invisible weight. He addressed Manich. "Open up your eyes, or you will miss the greatest experience of your life, my boy." Then looking up to his audience he said, "the first Round will only be a minor experience for this challenging patient because he will try not to look at what is happening. He will, however, be unable to resist one or two quick peeps, and that will be enough to prepare him for the next Rounding step in one week's time. Furthermore, the bright scarlet colour of his closed eyelids which he sees under the influence of H-S-4 will become unbearable, and he will open his eyes towards the end of the operation."

Beads of sweat appeared on Manich's brow. He tried to scream, but his muscles would not work for him. The pain in his foot was intense, and he found himself wishing they would cut it off. He even began to imagine that they were taking it off, and then he started to sob. Doctor Foote made a signal to a nurse, and Manich's leg was raised to a vertical position. The nurse fitted a tourniquet loosely around the leg just below the knee. Foote addressed his audience again.

"I take it that you are acquainted with the scores of amputational techniques that have been tried since Leonidas of Alexandria invented the flap in 200 A.D. My method rests heavily upon the tricks we have learned from such great surgeons as Gritti-Stokes, Chopart, Lisfranc to name only a few. The great art which Professor Klinger heralded was the sculpturing of the bone in such a way that it continued to grow in the months, sometimes years after the operation, so that it filled out the conical shape of the Round, the flaps having been packed especially to stretch evenly with the growth. It's a practice which you'll discover takes years to master. However, today, it is made much easier by the array of mechanical saws and scalpels that are available. I shall be using two such devices that I have developed primarily for step-wise Rounding."

He gestured toward an assistant who handed him a long glass box, which Foote held against Manich's straight leg as though measuring it for size. It was sealed all around, except for one end, to which was attached a stainless steel metal frame, with two big handles on either side. Foote turned a latch, and the frame came away. He then proceeded to slip the glass box onto Manich's leg, so that his foot and leg were encased half way up the shin. The metal frame Foote held by one handle, and pulled a trigger, causing it to swing open. A nurse handed him a small pellet, which he slid into a cylinder at the side of a frame. He continued with his lecture.

"This apparatus we call an M-P-G, which is an abbreviation for Miniature Power Guillotine, and it has been developed purely for step-wise Rounding. Remember, the emphasis on this procedure is upon dramatizing the separation. I fit the machine back on to the glass box like this and adjust it so that it's in position at the part of the leg we desire to amputate. I have placed an explosive pellet into the chamber of the M-P-G, so that when I pull the trigger, a tiny blade of hardened steel is propelled faster than a bullet, and severs the limb in one thousandth of a second. Here we go, we have it in place. Nurse! Lower his leg, tighten the tourniquet. Any questions so far?"

"Yes, sir. Why the glass box?"

"I'm getting to that. The glass box is called a Preservation Box. You see, one of the important aspects of step-wise Rounding treatment is the conservation of the severed limbs. We waste as little as possible. Under the old flap method, a lot of tissue was discarded. The preservation box—you see the tube running into the end of it— will build up pressure inside, so that as soon as the M-P-G is fired, the box automatically seals itself, and the high pressure inside prevents loss of blood from the severed leg, so that it does not lose its shape by the time it gets to our preservation specialists. Now, I think we are ready. Oh, one more thing. All the old methods have been directed almost entirely to the prevention of any loss of blood. Whilst, of course, it is not safe for a patient to lose too much, the unique tourniquet that you see allows for split-second adjustment. In order to heighten the patient's experience, we loosen it just before firing the M-P-G. In this way, if we time it in unison with the pulse beat, the patient can be treated to the exciting spectacle of seeing his blood spurt across the room. We allow one spurt only and then tie down the tourniquet. Now, I think we are ready to—"

"Doctor?"

"What is it?"

"Doctor, if you want the patient to observe a spectacle, why not devise a method where you only take off the flesh, which a preservationist could later stuff so that the patient would be left with the spectacle of seeing his leg as an actual skeleton?"

"Who is asking this question?" Foote was clearly upset.

No one answered, but muffled sniggers could be heard over the intercom. Foote went red in the face and persisted. "That was not very funny. The operating room is no place for smart questions. This is a very serious procedure. We are dealing with a person, a patient. His whole life depends on us. We are shaping his future. It is not the time to be making wisecracks over his prostrate body. I expect the student who asked the question to apologize to me personally after the operation. Now, let's get down to work."

An assistant gripped one side of the M-P-G with both hands, while Foote took the other. The half dozen people in the theatre sprung to life.

"Pulse! Blood pressure!" Numbers called out in quick succession. Foote spoke again.

"I will now begin the counting, and on ten, release the tourniquet for half a second. That clear nurse?"

"Yes, Doctor!"

"One, two, three, four. Mister Manich, open your eyes, it's time! Seven—"

Manich kept his eyes tightly closed and held his breath. His heart pounded in his mouth, and he began to whimper again.

"—nine! Ten!"

There was a loud crack! Manich's eyes were jolted open and, aghast, he caught a glimpse of his blood spurting momentarily across the surgery. He heard a clatter of feet on the surgery tiles, someone walking away with his foot in a box. Manich wondered if he imagined it. No pain. Pain all gone. "Come back foot! Come back!"

"Clip! Clamp! Come on, I haven't got all day!" Foote spat out his orders.

"Pulse, one, two—"

Doctor Foote worked feverishly for some minutes, tying off the vessels. He held his hand out to the side. "Scalpel!" he ordered.

Foote probed into the lesion a little, then stood up straight to look up once more to address the spectators. "Now, this is the most tedious and challenging part. You see, because the old flap methods did not have to preserve the tissue of the severed leg, they could cut down into the section using all sorts of methods. With the straight M-P-G cut, this is avoided. Now, I must make careful incisions into the flesh, tease out the fibre, muscle and fat tissue, to form a Round over the bone. Sometimes it is necessary, if the bone is too large, to cut into and around the bone, and nip a little off the end. I must also carefully separate the flesh from the skin to a few inches above the cut, so that I may stretch the skin down to give the Round a smooth exterior. Get comfortable in your seats. This will take about three or four hours."

"Doctor?"

"Yes?"

"Doctor, I have heard the criticism that this method produces a flat unsightly Round, which may become miss-shaped with age. What do you say about that?"

"It depends, of course, what you mean by "unsightly." Frankly, I think that the flatter simpler Round is more in keeping with today's less ostentatious way of life. As far as the aging is concerned, we have just completed a follow-up study of all patients leaving the sanatorium over a ten year period, and no evidence of miss-shaping has been found. Now, let me get down to business. Scalpel! Mister Manich, why not take a peek? Open your eyes and see how lucky you are!"

*

In three weeks, Manich's Round had healed. He had put on one more fit of rage, this time when he realized that the injections he was having were beginning to localize pain in his left hand. Why must they take it from him? He had screamed at them, flung himself off the bed. Foote had ordered him tied down again. And most of the time since then, Manich had just lain there, staring blankly into space, hardly acknowledging the presence of the continuous flow of nurses and assistants who were conducting the usual preliminary tests. But then, Manich became aware of a soft, cultured voice penetrating the bustle and noise of the room. He recognized it immediately as Professor Klinger's.

"I thought I should do as the Cabinet recommended, and call in to check on the patient," Klinger was saying.

"Yes, of course, Professor Klinger, you are more than welcome," replied Foote, confident on his own territory. "Does the Chief Prosecutor know you are here?"

"What does that have to do with it?"

"Oh, nothing. Nothing at all. I just thought that I should have submitted a progress report by now."

"And how is the patient?"

"Come and see for yourself," Foote smiled proudly, taking Klinger by the arm.

He pulled down the bed covers, exposing Manich's bare, shortened body. Foote adjusted his stance as though preparing for a golf shot, then with quite a flourish, lifted the gauze from the newly Rounded leg. Klinger remained expressionless. There was no denying that it was an excellent surgical job. He gently slid his fingers to the side of the stump and felt for the scar. There was nothing to feel. Brilliant piece of work! How unfortunate that Foote was so misguided! Klinger stepped backward and slid his hands into the pockets of his red Doctor's gown. Walking across to the window, he gazed out, his eyes shifting spasmodically as they picked up various patients and followed them as they were wheeled about the hospital garden. Klinger had not wanted to come today. In the four weeks since the Cabinet meeting, he had tried to neutralize his unease, a sense of disenchantment he supposed, which had begun to enshroud his life. He had thrust himself into his practice, working day and night at the Great Hospital, hoping that these twinges would recede into the background. But they had not only remained, but they had also begun to gnaw at him at the most unexpected times. Sometimes he would be looking across at a stranger over a cup of coffee, and he would find himself wondering about her or his Rounding history. "Is she really happy?" he would wonder when he saw someone laughing heartily. And at the climactic moment of the Round unwrapping ceremony, he would find himself not feeling his usual pride in his art, but would be looking at the Round, feeling as though he had never seen one before. And the more he concentrated upon this experience, the more foreign Rounds seemed to become. To think that something he had considered beautiful for so long—

"Well, Professor Klinger?" Foote asked, smiling broadly, as he crossed his arms and stood back on his heels. Klinger pursed his lips and breathed in deeply.

"Doctor Foote, you are no doubt a very talented surgeon—"

"But?" Foote interjected.

"I'm sorry, Foote, but although your surgery is brilliant, I think your procedural treatment is nothing but refined butchery."

Foote's jaw dropped. He had never heard Klinger speak so bluntly.

"Old ways must make way for new, Professor."

"Because they are new, doesn't make them right. Old ways are tried and sure. Didn't you ever hear that?"

"Sarcasm doesn't become you, Doctor Klinger."

Klinger looked away. He stuck his tongue against his cheek and made a clucking noise. Turning back again, he looked past Foote and spoke, "Foote, I had better leave. There's no point in going on with this discussion. We both know that neither of us will change our position."

His voice trailed away. Foote coughed sharply and walked around to the other side of Manich's bed. He took out his stethoscope and listened to Manich's chest. Then he issued the commands.

"Nurse! Another ten mils of H-S-4! Bring in the trolley! We go to surgery in twelve minutes." He looked at his watch, as he picked up Manich's left hand and scrutinized it. Manich let out a little whimper. The doctor reassured him. "Don't worry, my boy. We'll take this pain off as quick as a wink!" He blinked his eyes and stroked Manich's sweating brow. "Nurse, bring a fresh towel for him."

"Can't you see what you're doing?" Klinger's voice crackled with anger and bitterness.

"Yes. I'm changing a repulsive, violent man into a beautiful, non-violent citizen."

"You are taking his life from him step by step!"

"I am Rounding him better than you or I. To say nothing of the unique, psychological experiences he's getting."

"You know no limits!"

"You think that of Madam President too?" Foote smirked as Klinger stepped past him and made for the door. Klinger stopped at the door and turned abruptly. He stared hard at Foote and hissed, "Yes!"

Foote stared back, stony faced. He was elated. He wanted to say something like, "You're too old, Klinger, go home and die." But he forced himself to be silent. This time, he would out-stare Klinger. The room fell silent, as though the earth had stopped rotating.

Suddenly, Klinger sniffed and looked down to the side of Foote's feet. He turned and left, and almost collided with the Chief Prosecutor in the doorway. But he pushed on, offering no recognition. The Chief Prosecutor paused, and watched bemused. Foote asked eagerly, "You heard it all?"

The Chief Prosecutor pretended not to hear. His leg clicked loudly as he walked across to Manich's bed. There was a brief scuffle as the nurses tried to cover up his Round. Foote called, "It's all right, nurse, His Honour Chief Prosecutor should see the work."

"It's not necessary," the Chief Prosecutor mumbled, "where is the nearest telephone?"

"Right down the hall."

The Chief Prosecutor left immediately. Foote signalled the attendants and Manich was trundled off to the operating room. Foote called out to the Chief Prosecutor.

"Excuse me, but I must operate right now. I have reserved a front seat for you in the gallery, Chief Prosecutor. Is that O.K.? I'll try to delay things as much as I can until you get there, so you won't miss the action."

The Chief Prosecutor did not answer. He was trying to call Madam Fantasmag, but there was no answer. With a puzzled look, he replaced the receiver carefully. He pulled his leg around and limped towards the elevator that would take him to the operating room gallery. He had never seen one of Foote's performances and was looking forward to it.

*

John Peters had been taken to a dungeon cell, although he was treated with every courtesy. Very soon, the door was unbolted, and the solid torso of Brutus filled the doorway.

"The most gracious Madam awaits you," Brutus announced with an affected Butler's accent. There was a dreamy, faraway look in his eyes. He handed Peters a white sheet to wrap around his body. Peters stepped into the passageway. There the Madam sat, poised on her most resplendent chair, bedecked in a flowing gown of gold and purple sequins, which covered her tiny body and the whole of the chair as well, and hung to the floor in big wavy pleats. Her eyebrows had been speckled with silver dust, her old teeth polished until they gleamed in the fluorescent light. Her mouth was sensuously painted bright scarlet, giving it a permanently puckering appearance. Her gray lines and wrinkles had disappeared beneath the handiwork of a skilled cosmetician. She had been a beauty in her time, thought Peters. Now the Madam spoke.

"Come, Brutus, no dawdling! It's time!" She looked at John Peters and scanned his shrouded body from head to toe. "Mr. Peters, would you wheel me please?" Brutus narrowed his eyes, and Peters complied. "And place your hand on my shoulder? No, a little higher, so your finger touches my neck. Yes, good. Brutus, go ahead and open door sixty-nine."

"But Madam! That's the door to—"

"I know! I know!" snapped the Madam, "I said open it! Do you dare question your benefactor?"

Brutus winced. She had never called herself his benefactor before. He turned to John Peters and sneered. The Madam persisted. "Brutus, open it!" He went ahead and opened a hidden door that was set into the red brick wall of the passageway. Peters' nostrils immediately quivered. The thick stench of sickly, fatty substance wafted out. They entered a dimly lit room, more like a vault, with a low ceiling, the walls almost in total darkness. Brutus closed the door behind them. The Madam spoke again.

"Mr. Peters, a little to the right please, that's right. Now, press that button." He did so, and a fluorescent light flickered on to illuminate a display case. "Mr. Peters, I want you to see me as I really am. I want you to know about me before you play your part. Brutus, leave us." The chains and medals jingled as Brutus moved, then hesitated at the door. "I said, leave us, Brutus."

"But Madam, he's a criminal!"

"How dare you, Brutus! You of all people! Leave us!" Brutus scowled and left making as much noise as possible. Peters felt ill at ease. He realized that it was in his power to actually kill this shrivelled up old hag. He looked up at the display case and gasped.

"Wonderful, isn't it? I'm pleased you are impressed. Let's get up closer, shall we? I'll tell you all about it."

John Peters stared horrified. The Madam continued in romantic and nostalgic tones. "This is when I was two years old. Hard to believe, isn't it?" she sighed. "A pity they hadn't developed the technique of perfect preservation that we have today. But it has a lot of character about it, doesn't it?"

Peters gulped. All he saw was a wrinkled up little toddler's arm, coloured the dirty gray of decayed shrunken flesh. It was bent slightly at the elbow, and the hand had apparently been set in a position to open out all the fingers, which, it seemed, had once been separated from the hand and was reattached. The socket at the other end had been tied with a pink bow, now faded. The Madam carried on.

"Next button, Mr. Peters." The next box lit up. "These were my birthdays. I had a finger or toe Rounded for each year until I was ten." She giggled, "I used to be so excited!"

Peters stepped around the chair to look at her. Her eyes were vacant, there was a happy smile on her face.

"Next! Next, quickly, Mr. Peters!" she ordered excitedly. "See what better curves it has? What fantastic progress we've made, Mr. Peters! Who would have thought that we could preserve our childhood, indeed our past, so realistically? Look at that! Just like the day I wore it! I was just fifteen at the time. Beautiful shape, don't you think?" She coyly glanced at Peters.

"Oh, yes, beautiful, ravaging!" humoured Peters, his eyes almost popping out as he stared at the shapely pretty pink leg of a teenager. The socket above the thigh was tied with pink satin and white lace. "Beautiful!" he muttered.

"Ah! But the next!" The Madam's voice was beginning to squeak with excitement. Peters switched on the next box. A fingerless arm appeared.

The Madam called out, "Oh, no! This isn't the one, I hardly remember it. Next! Next!"

Peters pushed her chair to the other side of the vault. He could see the reflections in the glass that it was a large display case. He flicked the switch. But as the fluorescent light flickered on, there were loud noises in the passage outside, shouts and muffled bangs. There was a crash as the door to the vault flew open, and the Chief Prosecutor came charging in, propelled at such speed that he capsized and fell headlong down the centre of the room. The Madam frowned, and her eyes seemed to focus again. She shouted, "Chief Prosecutor! What are you doing?"

At the same time, Brutus stumbled in, bleeding heavily from the mouth, and cried, "Madam, I'm sorry! I tried to stop him, but he forced his way!"

The Madam persisted, "Prosecutor! What's the meaning of this?" Is nothing sacred anymore?"

The Chief Prosecutor, unstable on his D-legs at any time, was unable to get up on his own. He rolled onto his side, and yelled, a maniacal gleam in his eyes, "Sacred? Sacred? You have the impertinence to say that, when you are showing this, this—" he pointed to Peters, "—criminal the most sacrosanct memories we—"

"Look! Look! Here it is!" Fantasmag shouted, ignoring the Prosecutor's frenzied laments. The Madam, impassioned and aroused, raised her voice to a squeaky, high pitch. "Remember, my Prosecutor? I was in my late twenties at the time, and you were, well, really, a precocious child. You devil!"

The Prosecutor looked away and groaned. There was a gurgling sound, and vomit gushed out of his mouth. The acid mixed into the sickly fatty smell of the dungeon and Peters felt queasy. But he was rooted to the spot. There before him were two pink young legs. One obviously a woman's, shapely, slender, but toe-less. The other, that of a young man, or mature boy, hair coursing all the way down, once-taut tendons showing at the back of the knee where it was bent and entwined around the girl's leg. The toes were spread out in lively positions, which accentuated the small bones on the top of the foot, giving the impression of strength. The thigh socket of the girl's leg was tied with black lace; the man's with shining brown leather and a gold buckle.

"Remember, Prosecutor? Remember? Oh! Those were the days!" She looked down briefly at the Prosecutor whose body was rocking spasmodically. Then she looked to Brutus who was holding his bleeding mouth with his one arm. "Brutus, see to our Prosecutor, I think he's choking, poor thing!"

The Madam looked away and shifted her eyes jerkily downward.

"Mr. Peters, I will call you John now that we know each other better. Take me out. We have," she hesitated and smiled, "a little business of our own to attend to."

"Shouldn't I come with you?" pleaded Brutus pathetically.

The Madam replied curtly, "You get the Chief Prosecutor out of here and lock up the vault."

Peters pushed the Madam forward, and they left.

The Chief Prosecutor struggled to stand, and Brutus leaned over as far as he could to help him. Using each other as supports, they struggled out, Brutus turning to lock the doors behind them.

"Brutus, what the hell's going on?" The Chief Prosecutor complained, "I never knew this room existed. Did you?"

Brutus looked away sullenly and pretended not to hear. The Chief Prosecutor persisted. "Well, did you? Answer me, you beast!"

"Yes, I did!" Brutus sniffed and frowned deeply.

"Why didn't you tell me about it?"

"You never asked."

"I had a right to know! In the future—"

"There'll be no future!" Brutus cut in with an air of finality. "I serve the Madam, not you!"

The Chief Prosecutor was incensed, and muttered, "Dim-witted spaniel! Take me to the telephone. Come on! Shake it up! I can see you are useless in protecting our President's welfare. You allow her in the company of a criminal, unattended. Idiot!"

"The telephone is there. The washroom around the corner." They had stepped out of the elevator. "Will that be all sir?"

"Yes! But see you don't leave the Palace! There are going to be some changes around here!"

Brutus scurried back to the elevator and emerged again on another floor that was carpeted in dark maroon. It was the Madam's private apartment. He breathed in deeply and sighed, then stopped abruptly when the jangle of his medals disturbed the silence. Carefully, he removed them from his armpit and placed them in his pocket. He stood still, looking ruefully about. How many years had he served this incredible woman?

He had lived his life entirely for her. Happily, had himself Rounded at her slightest whim. Her every wish he had fulfilled, her every need satisfied. Brutus limped forward to the door facing him and stretched out his hand to touch the satin covered door knob, but he suddenly pulled his hand back as though it had been burned. Putting his hand on his face, he squeezed the bridge of his broad nose between his thumb and forefinger. His eyes were moist, and his hard shook as he retreated back to the elevator and pressed the button to take him down to the vaults.

*

At the Madam's direction, Peters turned the key in the lock and placed it on a small silver chain around the Madam's neck. She then directed him to drop the shroud that Brutus had given him and to stand naked before her.

"Stand close so I can touch you," she cackled. But because Madam Fantasmag had no arms or legs, it meant that Peters had to get up very close, almost astride the wheel chair, so that she was able to bend her head forward just enough to touch him with her tongue. She licked the pubic hair line, then sat back and laughed asthmatically. She looked him in the face, a glint of mischief in her eyes. Peters returned her glance, and at that moment he seemed to understand his role in this puzzling affair. He was now no longer afraid of her, though he had there and then decided that she was mad, completely mad. This had been their first meaningful communication, a fateful exchange. Fantasmag thrust her head forward again, and as best she could try to purr with her cackling voice.

"Mr. Peters, place me on the bed, please."

Peters turned to look at the strangely shaped bed, a bed with a raised portion in the middle. He turned his head back to catch a glimpse of the Madam. The glint remained in her eyes. He looked back at the bed. The raised portion, he now understood, was specially shaped to receive her fully Rounded torso. He noticed that above the bed there was a strange assortment of leather straps, pulley wheels, buckles and wooden bars. The Madam saw him looking at them.

"Those are my aids," she smiled proudly. "Haven't you ever wondered how totally Rounded persons manage? The leather frame is called a Rounder's Harness." Her voice cracked as she coughed loudly, then continued, "you won't need any of that, though." Her smile waned as she stared at him intensely. "Put me on the bed!" she commanded once again.

Peters looked back slyly. He felt cold, detached. "I could kill you," he mused aloud.

"But you won't," Fantasmag wheezed.

Peters darted quickly forward and placed his hands roughly around the Madam's throat. But the Madam continued to speak:

"You have touched me! A grave mistake, my boy! Don't you feel already soiled? Is it I or is it you?" she asked rhetorically, then laughed again. Peters frowned, not sure he had understood. But he loosened his hands and stepped back, holding them away from him as though they were wet or dirty.

"You have lost your innocence, child!" the Madam chided. "It started when you thought to kill me! Now you can never do it with certainty!"

"Stupid, crazy witch! I have two arms, two legs, and I'm a quarter your age! And you say I couldn't kill you with certainty?"

In a grand gesture, he lunged forward and snatched the Madam out of the chair as though she were just a poodle, then dropped her roughly on the raised bed.

"Well, why do you hesitate?" she mocked. "Why don't you do it?"

Peters turned his head quickly when he thought he heard scuffling at the door, and retreated from the bed to listen. But all was silent. He kept looking away as Fantasmag berated him.

"Why do you wait? Are you even afraid to look now?"

Peters remained motionless. The Madam coughed raspingly, causing him to look sideways. She made a smacking sound with her lips and wheezed again, "take off my clothes!"

Peters crossed his arms over his chest and retreated to a corner of the room.

"So you're a quarter my age?" the Madam jibed again, "that makes you better than me?"

Peters turned angrily. "I'm better than you because my body has not been mutilated," he snarled.

"Disgustingly unRounded," she quipped.

"You are not all there," mocked Peters.

"I have discarded unnecessary appendages."

"Unnecessary appendages! You're blind, old witch, blind! What about these? These abortive contraptions?"

Peters waved his hands dramatically towards the harnesses hanging above the bed.

"They obviate the necessity of arms and legs."

"But they're not a part of you!"

"Thank goodness! I can change them when they bore me."

"My arms and legs don't bore me! I love my arms and legs." Peters almost pleaded with her.

"Rubbish! You don't love things you take for granted! Have you ever thought what you could do without them?"

Peters stepped closer to the bed and stared at the shrunken torso as it wriggled to fit more snuggly into the raised bed.

The Madam flashed her eyes at him. "You never thought of it because you took them for granted. But now——"

"Utter crap! Utter crap!" Peters replied angrily, as he lurched forward and ripped off her clothes with one swift tug.

His eyes bulged, and he licked his lips nervously when he saw her mutilated body. But he collected himself enough to pursue his point.

"Look at yourself!" he shouted. "That's if you're able! Your body is the mutilated remains of a vivisected life. It's not Rounded, it's half destroyed!"

But the Madam laughed raucously. "You wanted to look all the time, didn't you? You succumbed again, you beautiful child!"

"I'm not a child," Peters complained unable to follow the twists and turns of the Madam's guile.

"But you are beautiful?" she jeered.

"In comparison to you, I have no doubt," he spoke with an undeniable touch of haughtiness.

"That is exactly what I thought!" The Madam studied him intensely, the pupils of her eyes growing darker.

"So?"

"So touch me!" she beckoned. "You need me!" The Madam smiled tenderly this time, showing her polished irregular teeth.

Silence. Peters came closer and looked down at her body. It began to wriggle and writhe as much as a torso can. He wondered if he weren't losing his mind, tried to understand what she had said. Her body, even if it were whole, would repulse him anyway. Her breasts hung like empty balloons. The skin across her abdomen seemed taut, like sun-drenched hide, barely covering her pelvic bones. The neck, the most repulsive to Peters, reminded him of the trunk of a cork tree. Yet he could not deny a strange fascination. This tiny collection of flesh, bones, and entrails; he wondered how such a heap of garbage could wield such power over so many, enter into the depths of everyone's lives, moulding them in its image.

But it was more than fascination. A chill on his back told him that he was sweating. He felt a dryness in the mouth, hotness behind the eyes, faint dizziness. He crawled up over the foot of the bed, moving gradually towards the raised pinnacle. Dropping his hands to his crotch, he squeezed the softness. He heard a whining, rattling noise above, and saw that the Roundman's harness had sprung to life, swaying, dipping, shaking. He raised his hands to his temples, digging the tips of his fingers into his hair. Head and shoulders were thrust back, spine arched, stomach and buttocks thrust forward. Somewhere afar he heard a shriek and muffled cries. It shook him out of his stupor, and he looked down at the Madam, now a savory object of his violence, which, he now understood with great clarity, he must consummate.

The Madam gave a deep sigh, and whispered, a satisfied smile on her face, "you too. Even you."

"Yes, even me," he said as he reached forward and placed his hand over her mouth and pushed so hard he could feel her crooked teeth pushing against her lips. She tried to open her mouth, but he pushed harder, clamping her mouth shut. "And now we shall not be even, but I shall conquer. " And with this solemn pronouncement full of vile and venom, he pinched her nose hard with his other hand, cutting off her life source, the air that she took for granted. With every spasm of his body, her torso shook as it never had before. Then as if on cue, the Madam's eyes widened, turned a pale shade of grey and stared up at the harness, which immediately rattled to a stop.

Peters reached up to one of the arms of the harness to pull himself up, but the steel rod came away in his hand. The machine was coming apart. And so it should, he thought to himself. He rolled off the bed, still clutching the steel rod. He looked for his clothes but could not find them. He couldn't remember how long he had been naked or where they must be. He glanced across at the Madam's remains, having to force down acid that came up from his stomach. He felt dirty, but he also felt powerful. It was a good combination, and he knew that once he got some clothes on, he would be unstoppable. He rummaged through closets and cupboards and finally found a red cape. It looked very much like the one that Dr. Klinger wore. Who knows, maybe he had been here too, Peters muttered to himself. In any case, it was just what he was looking for.

He was about to go out the way he came in when there was banging on the door, as though someone was trying to force entry. The steel rod in his hand, he ran across and opened the door. Brutus and McQuay the Prosecutor rushed in, the extent to which they were able to rush, that is. Peters stood amused awaiting their onslaught. They lurched at him, he dropped down and swiped his rod at each of their D-legs, and down they flopped. He stepped over to them, placing his foot on the Prosecutor's chest, and digging the steel bar into Brutus's throat.

"From now on," Peters said in a voice of authority, "you two work for me. The Madam bequeathed her Presidency to me."

Brutus and McQuay strained to take in the still torso of the Madam on the bed and the broken down harness.

"That's right. She's expired," spoke Peters a slight smirk at the corners of his mouth. "She passed everything—and I mean everything—on to me."

"But I served her for many years," whimpered Brutus, "I did everything she wanted."

"You'll never get away with this," threatened the Prosecutor.

"But I already have. And you two will help me carry it off. Unfortunately, you are both too well rounded to serve me in any ministerial capacity. I will appoint only unRounded ministers. But you will head up a special department, that of security and safety and will enforce the new law against stepwise rounding that will take effect immediately."

"And Constance, your only love you once told me, what about her?"

Peters looked across to the Madam then looked down on the Prosecutor, shifting for a moment all his weight on to his chest. "I will not tell her anything of this. Nor will you, if you love your daughter, as you have told me you do many times." He stepped back and held out his hand to help them stand.

Brutus commissioned a beautiful golden casket, a perfect cube, for Madam Fantasmag. Her body was embalmed and placed inside the cube, one side made of glass, and it was put in her museum, serving as the climactic piece for the visitor who followed the exhibit of the many parts of her long and productive life.

For his part, Peters was surprised how smooth everything went. He took care to ensure that Brutus and McQuay performed their duties in absolute secrecy. They worked only at night in unmarked ambulances, quietly picking up stray individuals who were step rounded, and placing them in the research hospital that President Peters had established, headed by none other than Dr. Foote. Peters had summoned him to the palace and asked him if he could find a way to re-attach limbs that had been cut off. Foote did not hesitate for one second. He assured the president that, if there was a way, he, Dr. Foote, would find it. He would only need sufficient resources and a good supply of patients for his trials. Peters responded accordingly, lecturing Dr. Foote that this was the only way to mend the terrible mistakes of the past. His high hope, of course, was that Dr. Foote may find a way to make Constance, the love of his life, whole again. There were a lot of possibilities, said Dr. Foote; stem cells, transplants, growing new legs from the embalmed legs that had been cut off. And if that didn't work, maybe a leg from someone else could be transplanted if it was a good match. Who knows? Anything was possible!

The only stick-in-the-mud was Dr. Klinger who, in spite of his tolerant, fair minded and even selfless character, could not find it in his heart to forgive Peters for wearing the robe he discovered in the Madam's closet. He was even prepared to accept the new regime, especially because he thought that Foote had gone too far with his stepwise rounding. So far, he knew nothing of Foote's swift adaptation to the new regime's demands. Going too far was Foote's exceptional talent. In any case, Dr. Klinger was happy enough to retire from his ministerial post and make way for younger, more energetic doctors, those who understood the intricacies of the unRounded. He even recommended one or two contenders for his position, both of them unRounded. He knew of them because he had declined to Round them when requested some years ago when they were teenagers, and he assumed that if he did not do it to such persons of respectable social position, no other surgeon would have touched them without informing him.

The most unfortunate and unintended (perhaps) outcome of the unRounded revolution (that is what the popular press called it) was the fortune, or misfortune more like it, of Mr. Manich. President Peters pardoned him of all offenses for which he had been convicted and even those for which he had been charged. President Peters ordered that all investigations of Manich and his followers cease forthwith, and in addition that the former prosecutor draw up an assessment of the compensation due him for the shocking invasion of his privacy and false charges laid against him. The Prosecutor, as cunning as ever, recommended a lifetime stipend for Mr. Manich and as well that every reasonable attempt is made to return him to his original, whole body, which meant reattaching two hands and two legs. Manich was not really consulted concerning this recommendation, though he was informed that the government intended to make him whole again and respectfully asked for his forgiveness for the damage done to him both financially and bodily. It would all be made up to him, and indeed, to demonstrate the government's good faith. He had been installed in a villa of some twenty rooms, including bathrooms and a clinic, with Brutus required to wait on him hand and foot (I apologize for this unseemly joke at Manich's expense, but the kind reader would agree, the entire situation demands it). The clinic, of course, was entirely furnished for Dr. Foote who would use Manich as his first guinea pig. There was the convenient fact that the amputations of Manich were very recent and that his severed limbs were frozen in Dr. Foote's massive freezer in which he stored every limb he had removed in anticipation of a day like the one that had now arrived.

The birth of a new society is an exciting event, not unlike the birth of a new star, or at least, that was the theme of President Peters' inaugural address. He tossed out the imagery of shooting stars, the amazing colours of the Northern lights, meteorites flying overhead, their new society a spaceship hurtling through space, brave, full of confidence. He promised a bold new future where all his people would be made whole again, and never more would people want that which they need not have. It would be a society of have-nots, in contrast to the society of haves that was. His press secretary (his lovely Constance) advised him that this terminology was way too abstract and would go over the heads of the people. But it was not so. Whether they understood it or not, they stood in rapturous attention and at the end applauded, at first quietly, then loudly finishing with cheers mixed with tears. The band struck up an uplifting tune taken from the marching song that good old England played each time a Governor arrived somewhere in its Empire, but it was soon dominated by the loud thumping of a bass drum by a drummer gone half mad because at last, he could use his unRounded leg to bang the pedal.

And so we leave this story of the death of a society and the birth of the new one on a wonderfully optimistic note. John Peters, the son of a nobody, had seen through the simple and quite stupid premise of a society that had grown self-satisfied and fell in upon itself like a sink hole in Florida once its unsustainable premise was exposed. Perhaps it was a coincidence that he found himself the chosen one by Madam Fantasmag, or perhaps it was by Her design. It's anybody's guess. What became immediately apparent, however, is that John Peters was an uncanny ruler, with a deft sense for what people wanted in life, and especially what they sought in a leader. He was all things to them and he actively every day made them whole again. To be made whole after feeling un-wholly, what more could one ask for in a life or of a ruler who made it so?

Postscript

As we know, the problem that faces all supreme leaders is how to transfer their power to the next generation, and worse, how to keep those immediately beneath them from rising up. President Peters quickly saw that he had made a mistake by firing all the old guard and replacing them with unRounded cronies. In the beginning, the latter was certainly loyal, but when they reflected on how quickly President Peters had usurped the throne, they were unable to put aside their own lust for power. Naturally, they saw in him a living example of what was possible. And when the President treated them to a tour of the Madam's vault it did not have the effect he anticipated. They were not overcome with awe at his accomplishments. On the contrary, they silently berated themselves for not having done what Peters did, since his solution of a little bit of violence seemed so obvious, even natural.

It took no time for President Peters to sense the envy that ran through his loyal staff. This worried him no end until late one sleepless night, standing alone in front of the Madam's gold cube, staring at her torso, the solution came to him, and he called an urgent meeting of his cabinet.

The next morning, the cabinet members entered the meeting room and were surprised to see Dr. Klinger, in his familiar red robe, sitting next to the President at the head of the oval table.

"Good morning," smiled the President.

"Good morning Mister President," they answered in unison.

"I want to welcome Dr. Klinger back to the cabinet and to thank him for coming out of retirement. You all know that, of the past regime, Dr. Klinger was the most brilliant and ethically outstanding individual ever to have served our society. I have asked him to return to duty briefly to oversee a new project that will move our society forward and ensure peace and harmony forever, well after each of us has passed on."

An assistant moved around the table, handing out a sheet of paper to each of the ministers who looked bemused, then squirmed in their seats as they began to read what was written. The President continued.

"I am passing around to you the draft text of a new edict I am issuing that will take effect at dawn tomorrow morning. It will require that all new-born babies, male or female, be circumcised."

"So why is Klinger here?" came an unexpected question.

"Dr. Klinger will direct this massive roll out of medical procedures. He is surely the best qualified.

"But he's part of that creep Fantasmag's entourage."

"Yes, I understand that of course. And I do acknowledge that our current Minister for Medical Procedures is more than capable of directing the operation. And certainly, much of the responsibility for the roll out will fall on her. But I need Dr. Klinger for another important task. I want to set an example for the people, so I require all my cabinet ministers to be circumcised, and Dr. Klinger is the only Doctor I would trust to carry out such an important procedure on such prominent individuals as yourselves."

A cloak of silence blanketed the room.

"We will begin with the Vice President tomorrow morning."

"But Mr. President!"

"All procedures will be televised. The meeting is adjourned."

Also by Colin Heston

9/11/TWO

This gripping novel offers a glimpse into the real world of counter terrorism, hints at why 9/11 was allowed to happen and warns us that it could easily happen again. It's politics as usual in New York City when Larry MacIver, world renowned criminologist, is tapped by NYC Mayor Ruth Newberg to save NYC from a second 9/11 attack. Will it be nuclear? Will it be bio? MacIver and his geeky assistant Manish Das must overcome FBI ineptitude, CIA intrigue and, most of all, the evil and ruthless Iranian terrorist Shalah Muhammud, to save the city. In the underground of this story, so suspenseful, so frustratingly funny at times, are the crucial questions of counter terrorism that worry anyone within a couple of hours drive from New York City: Will it be a drone next time? Will New York politics doom the city's defences? Written before drones were widely in use, the novel seems prescient of much that has happened (should and should not have happened) in the world of counter terrorism.

Miscarriages

Teen Chooka grows up in the weird world of 1950s Aussie pub life. When his alcoholic dad dies, he searches for his identity, and that of his shadowy underage girlfriend, Iris. Captivated by the pub's many crazy customers and their raucous stories, Chooka becomes a boozer just like them. But Iris, after a miscarriage, disappears and Chooka sets out on a search that takes him to foreign places including Melbourne university and Vietnam. The search ends in a Melbourne pub, where they start over, but this time there's a different ending.

"…a brilliant, unforgettable book about real people…a sensitive, touching and poignant story." - *Reader's Favourite.*

Ferry to Williamstown

In this raucous Aussie story, corpses pop up in the Yarra river while Lizzie entertains her powerful and kinky clients in her Winnebago, parked on the ferry to Williamstown. Tightly bound Detective Striker, confronted by the mob of Catholics, wharfies and communists who rule Williamstown, struggles to solve the mystery. Lizzie gets engaged to her uncle Bobby, the lame ferry driver, and her mum, Babs, spellbound by the strange Father Zappia, tries to solve her own mystery of St. Robert's toe. She throws a raucous send-off party for Lizzie, and out of the chaos emerge many truths.

About the Author

Colin Heston is the pen name of a criminologist of international repute, so he knows something about the world of crime and terrorism. In addition to 9/11 TWO, his published fiction includes *Miscarriages* (2018 US edition, 2019 Australian edition), and his first book of short stories *The Tommie Felon Show* (2018). His next novel, *Ferry to Williamstown*, a subcultural comic mystery set in Williamstown Australia. As a criminologist, Heston has written nonfiction books on the history of punishment and torture, edited a four volume encyclopedia on *Crime and Punishment around the World* and forthcoming, *Civilization and Barbarism: Punishing Criminals in the 21st Century* (May, 2020). .

HARROW AND HESTON
Publishers

AUSTRALIA, NEW YORK & PHILADELPHIA